Critical Praise for *B*

- A *New York Times* Editors' Choice
- A *Chicago Reader* Critic's Choice
- A selection of the *Essence Magazine* Book Club
- A selection of the Black Expressions Book Club

"Moody, lyrical prose reminiscent of Toni Morrison's *Beloved* . . . Though the fictional Abigail exists only on the pages of Abani's novella, her character will seize the imagination of everyone who reads her story."

—*Essence Magazine*

"Abani is a fiction writer of mature and bounteous gifts . . . *Becoming Abigail* is more compressed and interior [than *GraceLand*], a poetic treatment of terror and loneliness . . . its sharp focus on the devastation of one young woman, has a deeper kind of resonance . . . Abani, himself incarcerated and tortured for his writings and activism in Nigeria in the mid '80s, writes about the body's capacity for both ecstasy and pain with an honesty and precision rarely encountered in recent fiction . . . This is a powerful, harrowing work, made more so because, while much of the narrative seems to be a vortex of affliction, Abigail's destiny is not inevitable. The small canvas suits Chris Abani."

—Sam Lipsyte, *New York Times Book Review*

"*Becoming Abigail,* a spare yet voluptuous tale about a young Nigerian girl's escape from prostitution is so hypnotic that it begs to be read in one sitting . . . Abigail is sensitive, courageous, and teetering on the brink of madness. Effortlessly gliding between past and present, Chris Abani spins a timeless story of misfortune and triumph."

—*Entertainment Weekly*

"A darkly poetic investigation into the past's deceptive hold over the present . . . Abani writes in dense, gorgeous prose. Abigail is not a creature of pity but inspiration."
—*The Nation*

"Compelling and gorgeously written, this is a coming-of-age novella like no other. Chris Abani explores the depths of loss and exploitation with what can only be described as a knowing tenderness. An extraordinary, necessary book."
—Cristina Garcia, author of *Dreaming in Cuban*

"Abani finds his place in a long line of literary refugees, from the Mexican revolutionary Ricardo Flores Magon to Bertolt Brecht and Theodor Adorno . . . *Becoming Abigail* is, not surprisingly, about memory, loss, and all the cruel disjunctions of exile. Not for a moment, though, does Abani allow himself that most tempting stupefacient of exile, nostalgia. Abani's prose is diaphanous and poetic. His lyricism is elliptical, almost evasive . . . *Becoming Abigail* is a hard, unsparing book, cruel in its beauty, shocking in its compassion."
—*Los Angeles Times Book Review*

"A lyrical yet devastating account of a young woman's relocation to London from Nigeria . . . Abani's abundant talent is clearly evident throughout, as is his willingness to be brutally honest without being grotesque. He also refrains from polemics and focuses solely on the artistic presentation of a young, tragic life, leaving interpretation to the reader."
—*Library Journal*

"Abani's voice brings perspective to every moment, turning

pain into a beautiful painterly meditation on loss and aloneness."
—Aimee Bender, author of *The Girl in the Flammable Skirt*

"A searing girl's coming-of-age novella in which a troubled Nigerian teen is threatened with becoming human trade . . . Recalling Lukas Moodysson's crushing *Lilya 4-Ever,* this portrait of a brutalized girl given no control over her life or body, features Abani's lyrical prose and deft moves between short chapters."
—*Publishers Weekly*

"Spare, haunting vignettes of exquisite delicacy . . . Never sensationalized, the continual revelations are more shocking for being quietly told, compressed into taut moments that reveal secrets of cruelty—and of love—up to the last page. Abani tells a strong young woman's story with graphic empathy."
—*Booklist*

"Abani's writing never becomes didactic—*Becoming Abigail* has the elegance and lyricism of a prose poem but doesn't soft-pedal the abuse it chronicles."
—*Chicago Reader*

"Abani's empathy for Abigail's torn life is matched only by his honesty in portraying it. Nothing at all is held back. A harrowing piece of work."
—Peter Orner, author of *Esther Stories*

"Abani writes in a fearless prose . . . He is able to toe that line between restraint and abundance, unfolding Abigail's history like the raising of a bandage."
—*Time Out Chicago*

Critical Praise for *GraceLand*

- Winner: 2005 Hemingway/PEN Prize
- Winner: 2005 Silver Medal, California Book Awards
- Winner: 2005 Hurston/Wright Legacy Award
- Finalist: 2005 *Los Angeles Times* Book Prize
- Shortlisted for the Best Book Category (Africa Region) of the Commonwealth Writer's Prize
- 25 Best Books of 2004: *Los Angeles Times*
- Best Books of 2004: *San Francisco Chronicle*
- Barnes and Noble Discover Great New Writers selection
- *New York Times Book Review* Summer 2004 "Vacation Reading/Notable Books" selection

"Extraordinary . . . This book works brilliantly in two ways. As a convincing and unpatronizing record of life in a poor Nigerian slum, and as a frighteningly honest insight into a world skewed by casual violence, it's wonderful . . . And for all the horrors, there are sweet scenes in *GraceLand* too, and they're a thousand times better for being entirely unsentimental . . . Lovely."
—*New York Times Book Review*

"Chris Abani's *GraceLand* is a richly detailed, poignant, and utterly fascinating look into another culture and how it is cross-pollinated by our own. It brings to mind the work of Ha Jin in its power and revelation of the new."
—T. Coraghessan Boyle, author of *Drop City*

"Abani's intensely visual style—and his sense of humor— convert the stuff of hopelessness into the stuff of hope."
—*San Francisco Chronicle*

"*GraceLand* amply demonstrates that Abani has the energy, ambition, and compassion to create a novel that delineates and illuminates a complicated, dynamic, deeply fractured society."

—*Los Angeles Times*

"A wonderfully vivid evocation of a youth coming of age in a country unmoored from its old virtues . . . As for the talented Chris Abani, his imaginary Elvis is as memorable as the original."

—*Chicago Tribune*

"*GraceLand* teems with incident, from the seedy crime dens of Maroko to the family melodramas of the Oke clan. But throughout the novel's action, Abani keeps the reader's gaze fixed firmly on the detailed and contradictory cast of everyday Nigerian life. Energetic and moving . . . Abani [is] a fluid, closely observant writer."

—*Washington Post*

"Abani has written an exhilarating novel, all the more astonishing for its hard-won grace and, yes, redemption."

—*Village Voice*

"Ambitious . . . a kind of small miracle."

—*Atlanta Journal-Constitution*

"It is to be hoped that Mr. Abani's fine book finds its proper place in the world . . . [Abani's] perception of the world is beyond or outside the common categories of contemporary fiction and he is able to describe what he perceives compellingly and effectively . . . [Abani captures] the awful, mysterious refusal of life's discrete pieces to fit."

—*New York Sun*

"An intensely vivid portrait of Nigeria that switches deftly between rural and urban life."

—*Boston Globe*

"Singular . . . Abani has created a charming and complex character, at once pragmatic and philosophical about his lot in life . . . [and] observes the chaotic tapestry of life in postcolonial Africa with the unjudging eye of a naïve boy."

—*Philadelphia Inquirer*

"Abani masterfully gives us a young man who is simultaneously brave, heartless, bright, foolish, lustful, and sadly resigned to fate. In short, a perfectly drawn adolescent . . . Abani's ear for dialogue and eye for observation lend a lyrical air . . . In depicting how deeply external politics can affect internal thinking, *GraceLand* announces itself as a worthy heir to Chinua Achebe's *Things Fall Apart*. Like that classic of Nigerian literature, it gives a multifaceted, human face to a culture struggling to find its own identity while living with somebody else's."

—*Minneapolis Star-Tribune*

"*GraceLand* is an invaluable document."

—*San Diego Union-Tribune*

"Remarkable . . . Chris Abani's striking new novel, *GraceLand*, wins the reader with its concept—an Elvis impersonator in Nigeria—and keeps him with strong storytelling and characterization . . . *GraceLand* marks the debut of a writer with something important to say."

—*New Orleans Times-Picayune*

Critical Praise for *The Virgin of Flames*

"Chris Abani reveals Los Angeles as we have never seen it before—magical and crumbling, a place of deserted rooftop oases and intersections where new identities are bought and sold. He has rewritten our American story and brought the world into our streets, our most private negotiations and confessions."

—Walter Mosley

"Ambitious and original . . . Abani's Los Angeles is at turns desolate and luminous . . . a place that is horrifying and tender and absurd in equal measure."

—*New York Times Book Review* (Editors' Choice)

"A powerful, scary, and beautiful novel. Abani is a force to be reckoned with, a world-class novelist and poet."

—Russell Banks

"Chris Abani is a force of nature. In the world of letters he is a luminous shattering talent, and *The Virgin of Flames* is his strangest and wildest trip yet."

—Junot Díaz

"Through symbolism both Catholic and apocalyptic, Abani lets his vast descriptive powers run wild."

—*Entertainment Weekly*

"You are bound to find yourself moved and entertained by an iridescent novel from a writer who has come through Lagos and London to take his place as one of our newest, and most gifted, native sons."

—*Chicago Tribune*

"With a command of Los Angeles' underbelly reminiscent of Walter Mosley at his most striking, Abani spirits his angst-ridden artist toward a breathtakingly unexpected, if perhaps inescapable, conclusion."

—*BookPage*

"What is most moving here is Abani's earnest love poem to this particular Los Angeles."

—*Los Angeles Times*

"Abani has established himself as an unflinching advocate for individuals exiled to society's underside . . . Redolent of the hunger and doom of Nathanael West, lush and surreal as L.A.'s street murals, and combustible with denied eroticism and thwarted spirituality, Abani's feverish portrait of a haunted artist embodies post-9/11 anxiety and the longing for peace."

—*Booklist*

"Our guide through this westernmost circle of the American hell . . . What is most arresting . . . isn't the grotesqueness Abani observes . . . but the pathos he unfailingly finds alongside it like a jewel in the muck."

—*Boston Globe*

"With its complex characters and exquisitely imagined cityscapes, *The Virgin of Flames* is the work of a top-notch writer."

—*Time Out New York*

Song for Night

Song for Night

a novella by

Chris Abani

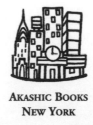

AKASHIC BOOKS
NEW YORK

This is a work of fiction. All names, characters, places, and incidents are the product of the author's imagination. Any resemblance to real events or persons, living or dead, is entirely coincidental.

Published by Akashic Books
©2007 Chris Abani

ISBN-13: 978-1-933354-31-6
Library of Congress Control Number: 2007926049

First printing
Printed in Canada

Akashic Books
PO Box 1456
New York, NY 10009
info@akashicbooks.com
www.akashicbooks.com

Also by Chris Abani

Novels
Masters of the Board
GraceLand
The Virgin of Flames

Novellas
Becoming Abigail

Poetry
Kalakuta Republic
Daphne's Lot
Dog Woman
Hands Washing Water

Of course, for Sarah

And my nephews—Ikenna, Obinna,
Chuks, Craig, Carl, Neven

We die only once, and for such a long time
—Molière

on any path that may have heart. There I travel
—Carlos Castaneda

Silence Is a Steady Hand, Palm Flat

What you hear is not my voice.

I have not spoken in three years: not since I left boot camp. It has been three years of a senseless war, and though the reasons for it are clear, and though we will continue to fight until we are ordered to stop—and probably for a while after that—none of us can remember the hate that led us here. We are simply fighting to survive the war. It is a strange place to be at fifteen, bereft of hope and very nearly of your humanity. But that is where I am nonetheless. I joined up at twelve. We all wanted to join then: to fight. There was a clear enemy, and having lost loved ones to them, we all wanted revenge.

If you are anything like Ijeoma you will say that I sound too old for my age. She always said that: said, because although her name in Igbo means Good Life, she died young, a year ago, aged fourteen, her wiry frame torn apart by an explosion. Since she couldn't speak either, it might be misleading to say *she said*, but we have developed a crude way of talking, a sort of sign language that we have become fluent in. For instance, silence is a steady hand, palm flat, facing down.

The word *silencio*, which we also like, involves the same sign with the addition of wiggling fingers, and though this seems like a playful touch, it actually means a deeper silence, or danger, and as in any language, context is everything. Our form of speech is nothing like the kind of sign language my deaf cousin studied in a special school before the war. But it serves us well. Our job is too intense for idle chatter.

I am part of a platoon of mine diffusers. Our job is to clear roads and access routes of mines. Though it sounds simple, our job is complicated because the term *access routes* could be anything from a bush track to a swath cut through a rice paddy. Our equipment is basic: rifles to protect against enemy troops, wide-blade machetes for clearing brush and digging up the mines, and crucifixes, scapulars, and other religious paraphernalia to keep us safe.

We were not chosen for our manual dexterity or because of our advanced intelligence, though most of us are very intelligent. We were chosen simply because we were small, slight even, and looked like we wouldn't grow much in the nutrition-lacking environment of a battlefield. We were chosen because our light weight would protect us from setting off the deadly mines even when we stepped on them. Well, they were right about the former, even now at fifteen I can pass for an average twelve-year-old. But they were so wrong about the latter. Even guinea fowl set off the mines. But they must have known: that is why they imposed the silence. I finger the scar on my throat that marks the cut that ended my days of speech.

There is a lot to be said for silence, especially when it comes to you young. The interiority of the head, which is a misnomer—misnomer being one of those words silence brings you—but there is something about the mind's interiority no less that opens up your view of the world. It is a curious place to live and makes you deep beyond your years and familiar with death. But that is what this war has done. I am not a genius, though I would like to be, I am just better versed at the interior monologue that is really the measure of age, of the passage of time. Why do I say this? Because when we say the passage of time we mean awareness of the passage of time, and when we say old, we really mean experienced. I know all this because my job requires me to concentrate on every second of my life as though it were the last. Of course if you are hearing any of this at all it's because you have gained access to my head. You would also know then that my inner-speech is not in English, because there is something atavistic about war that rejects all but the primal language of the genes to comprehend it, so you are in fact hearing my thoughts in Igbo. But we shan't waste time on trying to figure all that out because as I said before, time here is precious and not to be wasted on peculiarities, only on what is essential.

I have become separated from my unit. I don't know for how long since I have only just regained consciousness. I am having no luck finding them yet, which is ironic given that my mother named me My Luck. But as Grandfather said, one should never stop searching for the thing we desire most.

And right now, finding my unit is what I desire most. We were all together, when one of us, Nebuchadnezzar I think it was, stepped on a mine. We all ducked when we heard it arming—that ominous clicking that sounds like the mechanism of a child's toy. The rule of thumb is that if you hear the explosion, you survived the blast. Like lightning and thunder. I heard the click and I heard the explosion even though I was lifted into the air. But the aftershock can do that. Drop you a few feet from where you began. When I came to, everyone was gone. They must have thought I was dead and so set off without me: that is annoying and not just because I have been left but because protocol demands that we count the dead and tally the wounded after each explosion or sweep. Stupid fools. Wait until I catch up with them, I will chew them out; protocol is all that's kept us alive. Counting is not just a way to keep track of numbers, ours and the enemy's, but also a way to make sure the dead are really dead. In training they told us to maximize opportunities such as these to up our kill ratio; for which we would be rewarded with extra food and money we can't spend. I like to pretend that I do it to ease the suffering of the mutilated but still undead foes, that my bullet to their brain or knife across their throat is mercy; but the truth is, deep down somewhere I enjoy it, revel in it almost. Not without cause of course: they did kill my mother in front of me, but still, it is for me, not her, this feeling, these acts. The downside of silence is that it makes self-delusion hard. I rub my eyes and spit dirt from my mouth along with a silent curse aimed at my absent comrades. If they'd checked they would have noticed that I wasn't dead.

The first thing I do is search for Nebu's body. That's the way it is laid out in the manual (although of course none of us has ever seen the manual but Major Essien drummed it into us and we know it by heart): first locate and account for friendly casualties, then hostiles; in that order—friend, then foe. The funny thing is, though I search, I can't find Nebu's body. There are no other bodies either, which means the enemy hasn't been around.

Let me explain something, which on the surface might sound illogical but isn't. We all lay land mines, the rebels and the federal troops, us and the enemy, but we do it in such a hurry that no one bothers to map these land mine sites, no one remembers where they are. That and the fact that territory shifts between us faster than sand tracking a desert, ground daily gained and lost, makes it hard to keep up. Given that the mine diffusers and scouts are always the advance guards, it is easy to see how minefields are often places where we intersect. In this case however it seems like there was no enemy, that Nebu simply got careless; or unlucky.

My first instinct is always survival so I abandon the search as quickly as I can and get out of the open. I debate whether to head for the river, fifty yards to my left, or the tree cover, seventy yards or so to my right. I choose the river. Rivers are the best way to keep close to habitation as well as the fastest means of travel. I hug the banks in the shadows and carefully observe any developments, of which I must confess there are very little. So far I haven't met anybody and I haven't found any traces of my unit. It is not good to be alone in a war for long. It radically decreases your chances of survival.

But my grandfather always said, "Why put the ocean into a coconut?"

Night Is a Palm Pulled
Down over the Eyes

It is dark: lampblack. The only points of light are flickering fireflies. Stupidly I fell asleep practically in the open, under a mango tree near the riverbank, amid the rotting fruit strewn everywhere. I lie still, waiting for all my senses to wake up to any possible danger, remembering how I came to be here, and realizing that I must have fallen asleep after feasting on too many mangoes. I strain and discern dim outlines to my left: the forest. Getting up, I walk across the dark spread of grass between the river and the forest, stopping at the edge of the tree line. The silence is absolute as though the forest has just sucked in its breath. Deciding I'm not harmful, it lets it out in the gentle noises of night. To ground myself, I run my fingers meditatively over the small crosses cut into my left forearm. The tiny bumps, more like a rash than anything, help me calm myself, center my breathing, return me to my body. In a strange way they are like a map of my consciousness, something that brings me back from the dark brink of war madness. My grandfather, a fisherman and storyteller, had a long rosary with bones, cowries, pieces of metal, feathers, pebbles, and twigs tied into it that he used to remember our genealogy. Mnemonic devices, he called things like this. These crosses are mine.

Filtering the dark into gray shadows, fingers still reading the Braille on my arm, I try to force my eyes to adjust, but my night vision is not very good. The forest isn't familiar territory despite years of jungle and war, and the silence is disconcerting particularly because for the past three years I haven't been alone at night. I have been in a pack with the other mine diffusers. Even then, we all relied on Ijeoma to guide us. She always knew the right thing to do, and the right time to do it. God knows I miss her, love her. *Loved* her. But I can't think about that now. I must move. I glance around me and sift my memory for ideas, guide points. I look up, thinking perhaps the stars will guide me, but there are hardly any and I have forgotten the names of the constellations and their relationships anyway. The only thing I can remember is the phrase, *follow the big drinking gourd home*. I try to make out the big dip of its shape, but clouds and treetops are occluding everything. Honing my fear to an edge, I step off, sinking into the depths of the forest.

I pause to light a cigarette, trying to make out the forest in the dying light: matches are too few and precious to be wasted solely for trying to see. I suck on the filter, singeing the tip into a red glow. In the distance I hear a nocturnal wood dove. I press on, crashing through the forest with the finesse of a buffalo. Bugs bite, sharp spear grass rip at my skin. It finally gives way to wetlands, the beginning of a swamp. The blood from my cuts attracts leechlike creatures that suck on my arms and feet as I splash deeper through what turns out to be a mangrove swamp. I must have traveled in a curve, following the forest back to where the river cut through it. I must have because that's the only way I can be trudging through a mangrove swamp. It is not fun but we passed a mangrove swamp on the way in yesterday, so I must be retreating the right way. Into safe territory.

I hate mangroves though. The trees skate the water on roots like fingers, so human and yet so hauntingly bewitched they terrify me. The water levels aren't uniform. Sometimes only ankle deep, sometimes thigh deep, sometimes the ground sheers away beneath my feet submerging me gasping in the chocolate thick brown water.

Exhausted, I find a tree with a few low-hanging branches and climb, high as I can, until the swamp and river below are no more than a black shimmer in the night. Building a nest of branches, something we learned from the monkeys, I tie myself carefully to the thickest one. We might have learned some tricks from the monkeys, but we aren't monkeys. Sleep is a two-by-four catching me straight between the eyes and knocking me squarely into oblivion. Rest though is another matter. I haven't rested since that night. There has been exhaustion; sleep even. But not rest. Not since my unit stumbled into a small village, or what was left of it, several huts falling apart at the edge of a bomb-pitted strip of tar. We saw a group of women sitting around a low fire, huddled like every fairy-tale witch we had been weaned on. Armed to the teeth with AK-47s and bags of ammo and grenades, mostly stolen from the better U.S.–armed enemy soldiers we had killed, but still wearing rags, we stood close together, watching the women, unsure what to do; or whether to approach. The women were eating and the smell of roasting meat drove us on.

"Good evening, mothers," we said, respectfully.

The women paused and cackled, but didn't reply, and why would they since they probably didn't understand our crude sign language. We noted that one woman, not as old as the others, was lying on the ground. She was bleeding from a wound to her head and looked dazed.

"May we have some food?" I asked. I was the unspoken, unranked leader of the troop. "We are brave warriors fighting for your freedom."

This time my gestures, pointing to the food and miming eating, seemed to be understood and the old women waved me over. I approached and reached down to the metal brazier with meat on it. I recoiled from the small arm ending in a tiny hand, and the tiny head still wearing its first down. It only took a minute for the women to calculate the cost of my alarm and revulsion, so that even as I was reaching for my AK-47, they were scattering in flight, not forgetting to grab onto bits of their gory feast. I emptied a clip into them, as my platoon cheered at the snapping of old bones and the sigh of tired flesh, even though they didn't know why I was killing the women. The woman holding onto the head let go as she fell and it hit the ground and rolled back toward me.

It is that little face, maybe a few months old, that keeps me from rest.

Death Is Two Fingers
Sliding across the Throat

Death is always the expectation here and when my throat was cut it was no different. Nobody explained it at first. Nobody had time; nobody cared; after three years of a civil war nothing is strange anymore; choose the reason that best satisfies you. There are many ways to say it, but this is the one I choose: they approached me and said I had been selected for a special mission. I had been selected to be part of an elite team, a team of engineers highly trained in locating and eliminating the threat of clandestine enemy explosives. Even though I had no idea what clandestine enemy explosives were, I was thrilled. Who wouldn't be after three weeks of training and all the time marching for hours in the hot sun doing drills with a carved wooden gun while waiting for the real thing—either from the French who had promised weapons or from the front, where they had been liberated from the recently dead. That was what determined your graduation date: when a gun could be found for you; ammunition was a luxury, sometimes it came with the gun, sometimes it didn't, but you had to graduate nonetheless.

Armed with our knowledge of marching in formation and with a sometimes loaded weapon, we were sent off to the rapidly shrinking front or to pillage nearby villages for supplies for the front. It didn't matter which, as long as you were helping the war effort. So when an officer approached me and said I had been chosen to be part of an elite team, I was overjoyed.

I should have been suspicious of the training. I mean I am a smart person; I grew up in a city, not like one of the village fools that hung around us and were baffled by the simplest things like how to open the occasional sardine tins we were lucky to get with the strange-shaped keys—especially as the tins didn't have keyholes. Stupid village and bush shits, almost as stupid as the northern scum we are fighting. How could I know what the training for diffusion of clandestine enemy explosives consisted of? But the officer was reassuring. *Major Essien* his name tag said. That he was an officer of considerable influence was reinforced by the fact that he was one of the few who had been in the actual army before the war, and he was one of the few who still wore a clean crisp uniform with gleaming brown boots: cowboy boots. We would later nickname him John Wayne, but I am getting ahead of myself.

This is how we were trained: first our eyes were made keen so we could notice any change in the terrain no matter how subtle: a blade of grass out of place, scuffed turf, a small bump in the ground, the sharp cut of a metal tool into earth—any sign of human disturbance to the ground soon became visible to us. The funny thing though is that as keen as our eyesight grew in the day, we were blinder than most at night. Ijeoma, who was smarter than all of us combined, said it had to do with the fact that we burned our corneas in the intense sunlight straining to see. I didn't know what a cornea was even though I was in secondary school when the war started; none of us did. So she caught a frog, squeezed its eyes from its head, and showed us.

Having trained our eyes, they began to train our legs, feet, and toes. We learned to balance on one leg for hours at a time, forty-pound packs on our backs in so many odd and different positions that we looked like flamingos on drugs, all the while supervised by John Wayne, who walked among us tapping a folded whip against his thigh. Whenever we faltered, that whip would snake out like it had a mind of its own, its leather biting deep and pulling skin with it.

And all the while he would chant: "This is from the manual, the same manual that they use in West Point, the same one they use in Sandhurst; the military manual for the rules of engagement—the rules of war, for want of a better phrase. These are rules even you can understand. Now move out and follow orders!"

Once, Ijeoma asked to see the manual. John Wayne looked at her for a long time.

"You are lucky I was trained in West Point, otherwise I would just blow your brains out for challenging me. But I am a civilized man. You want to see the manual? It is here"— he tapped his forehead—"that way it can never be lost, nor we. We can never be lost as long as we follow the manual. The manual is like the rules of etiquette for war. Follow the protocols I shall show you from it and you will survive. As for seeing it, the only way that can happen is if you split my head open. Do you want to split my head open?"

Ijeoma shook her head.

"Good. If you don't want me to split your head open, you should follow orders!"

That was that. We followed orders, did what we were told, even when the training seemed at odds with what we thought soldiers should know, like the feet exercises, mostly from ballet. To make our feet sensitive, we were told, which was funny because we weren't going to be issued boots. The rebel army didn't have any, but even if we did, we wouldn't get them because they needed our toes to be exposed all the time. Then we were taught to use our toes almost like our fingers. One exercise which was cruelly ironic was tying our training officer's shoelaces with our toes.

Having learned to walk across different terrain with my band of fellow elite, feeling for the carefully scattered lumps in the ground, being careful not to step on them as per instruction, clearing the earth around the buried mines with our toes, we learned to bend and insert a knife under the firing mechanism and pull out the valve. We practiced on live mines and we realized the value of the one-legged balancing when we accidentally stepped on one, arming it. We balanced on one foot, reached down, and disabled the mine. We were discouraged from helping each other in these situations—if things went wrong it was better to lose one instead of two mine diffusers, John Wayne explained, almost kindly.

A week before graduation he took us all into the doctor's office. One by one we were led into surgery. It was exciting to think that we were becoming bionic men and women. I thought it odd that there was no anesthetic when I was laid out on a table, my arms and legs tied down with rough hemp. John Wayne was standing by my head, opposite the doctor. I stared at the peculiar cruel glint of the scalpel while the doctor, with a gentle and swift cut, severed my vocal chords. The next day, as one of us was blown up by a mine, we discovered why they had silenced us: so that we wouldn't scare each other with our death screams. Detecting a mine with your bare toes and defusing it with a jungle knife requires all your concentration, and screams are a risky distraction.

What they couldn't know was that in the silence of our heads, the screams of those dying around us were louder than if they still had their voices.

Memory Is a Pattern Cut into an Arm

I wake up confused. It is dark and I have to remind myself it is still the same night. As soon as I can, I should make some kind of calendar. The branches I am sleeping in are safe but uncomfortable. I can't place the sound that has woken me at first, but there it is again: the soft *put-put* of a motor. Carefully I look through the net of leaves and see a small motorboat gliding past. There are several men sitting in it, all heavily armed. One is in the prow operating a small searchlight that is sweeping the banks. They are all smoking, and from the smell of the tobacco I can tell it is top-grade weed. I inhale deeply, cautious not to make any noise. God I could use some of that weed; my head is pounding. It is an enemy vessel; but it could just as easily have been taken over by one of us rebels. Although, since the men in the boat are searching for anyone hiding in the water or the thick grass on the shore, it is unlikely. Not because we are not capable of it, but because this was most recently rebel territory and we wouldn't be killing our own, and murder is clearly the intent of the search. Unsettled, I rub my arm as I watch the boat circle under me then move on. It only lasts for a few moments but it feels longer.

As they depart, I reach for my knife. If Nebu had survived the explosion—which was unlikely since he was standing right over the mine when it went off, and so took the full
blast—he couldn't get far, wounded as he must be. Without
a doubt the patrol I have just seen will find him and finish
him off. With my knife tip I cut a small cross into my arm
for Nebu, wincing as the blood blisters up. I reach behind
me and cut into the tree and collect sap with the knife tip
and smear it into the small cut. It should help with the heal-
ing, I think, but almost immediately it starts to burn and I
know this is not a good thing, so I take out my prick and piss
all over my arm, feeling it stinging and cooling at the same
time. In basic first aid they told us that human urine is the
best field disinfectant there is. Holding my arm out, I let it
dry in the slight breeze. I reach for a cigarette and light it. I
am high enough that the men in the boat won't notice, even
if they come back.

In the dim glow from the cigarette, the crosses on my
arm look exactly like what they are: my own personal cemetery. I touch each cross, one for every loved one lost in this
war, although there are a couple from before the war. I cut
the first one when my grandfather died; the second I cut
when my father died, with one of his circumcision knives.
My father the imam and circumciser who it was said
betrayed his people by becoming a Muslim cleric and moving north to minister; and all this before the hate began.
The third I cut for my mother who died at the beginning of
the troubles that led to the war. The rest I have cut during

the war: friends, comrades-in-arms. With the one I just cut for Nebu, there are twenty in total. Eighteen are friends or relatives, as I said, but two were strangers. One was for the seven-year-old girl I shot by accident, the other for the baby whose head haunts my dreams.

I turn over my right forearm. There are six X's carved there: one for each person that I enjoyed killing. I rub them: my uncle who became my stepfather, the old women I saw eating the baby, and John Wayne, the officer who enlisted and trained us and supervised our throat-cutting and our first three months in the field, the man who was determined to turn us into animals—until I shot him.

"I shot the sheriff," I mumble under my breath, mentally walking through my memories, examining each one like a stranger walking through my own home, handling all the unrecognizable yet familiar objects.

It was a Wednesday. How I remember that detail is unclear given that nearly all my memories are mixed up, as though I have taken a fall and jumbled the images: probably a result of concussion brought on by the explosion. Wednesday, late afternoon: and the sky heavy with dark clouds. The muted light that fell like a hush was darkened by the deep green of foliage to one side, the red unpaved road scarring the middle, and to the other side a clearing covered with the gleam of white gravel and a church, not much more than a low whitewashed bungalow with a cross atop its corrugated iron roof, half of which had collapsed—maybe from a shell or a mortar, it was hard to tell. Another bungalow, the

priest's house, was off to the back, set close to the encroach-
ing greenery. In the front of the church was a battered pickup
truck that was idling in the shade of a tree. A white priest,
neck and face red against his white soutane, sat in the cab. In
the shadow of the bombed-out church, two women were
washing a statue of the Virgin with all the tenderness of a
mother washing a child. A seven-year-old girl played in the
gravel by their feet. I stared at that sight unbelievingly. Of all
the things they could have salvaged, I remember thinking.
Just then, a man came round the corner carrying a statue of
Jesus, cradled like a baby. I fought tears. There was something matter-of-fact about it all that was heartbreaking.

John Wayne stopped us with a casual wave, and we
spread out wordlessly into the formation we had been
trained to. The people in the church tableau froze as we
approached: the man holding Jesus, the women washing the
Virgin, and the priest in the truck whom I assume meant to
carry the statues to another church or parish where they
would be safe. As we moved forward in a loose fan that
tapered into a point, with John Wayne leading, only the
child moved. Smiling, she ran toward us. John Wayne bent
down, arms spread, a father home from work, except he
didn't look like a father, more like a bird of prey. He picked
up the seven-year-old girl and held her to his side.
Something about him in that moment must have terrified
her though because she began to cry.

"What is your name?" he asked her.

"Faith," she said, still crying.

John Wayne touched her face tenderly, and then when she smiled tentatively through her tears, he threw his head back and laughed.

"This one is ripe. I will enjoy her," he said, looking right at me, as though he expected me to challenge him, like I did the first time he had forced me at gunpoint to rape someone, but whatever he saw in my eyes made him laugh even louder. Without thinking, I lifted my AK-47 and opened fire. He moved, instinctively I think, the way an animal will, to escape the shot, and the bullet went through the seven-year-old and found John Wayne's heart. They both looked at me, faces wide with shock for a long moment, then John Wayne fell, taking the girl with him. Everyone scattered for cover, the women, the man carrying Jesus, still carrying Jesus, and the rest of the platoon; everyone except Ijeoma, who stood behind me, and the priest, who leapt out of his car and ran toward John Wayne and the girl.

Without a word the priest bent down, said a prayer over the child, kissed her forehead, and drew a cross in the air above her with two fingers. He pried her from John Wayne's arms and held her to his chest, her blood staining his white soutane. He seemed confused, unsure what to do next, and his eyes locked on mine were filled with tears and an expression I have seen too many times. He opened his mouth to speak but nothing came out. I was numb to John Wayne's death. Gladness would come later. For now, all I could think was that the only real casualty was Faith.

I became aware that Ijeoma was rubbing my back gently.

Without a word I turned and put my head on her shoulder. When I looked up, the rest of the platoon was gathered in a circle around us. Nebu had unpinned John Wayne's rank insignia and was holding it in his hand like a burning coal. He approached me silently and pinned it to my shirt, saluted, and turned around. The rest of the platoon came to full attention and saluted. I was now the leader, months into the war; our war.

I turned to Ijeoma. She looked at me with a mocking smile, then we all set off. In the weeks to come, we would see the old women eat the baby and Ijeoma would die.

Perhaps I should change my name to Unlucky.

Perhaps this is karma.

Perhaps this is how we learn love.

I wonder what Grandfather would have made of it.

Imagination Is a Forefinger
between the Eyes

Hiding is all I seem to do: from myself, from the enemy. But doubt never leaves, not even here in this tree. Like a spider busy spinning a web, my mind weaves the night into terror.

What does it mean to hide in a ceiling, in that narrow hot crawl space crouched like an animal smelling my own scent, full of it and grateful for it, while my mother stays below, in what seems like the brightest sunlight although it is only the light of a sixty-watt bulb, waiting to deflect the anger of people intent on murder, my murder, waiting so that I may live, and I watch what happens below and I am grateful that I can smell my smell, smell my smell and live while below me it happens, it happens that night bright as day, but I cannot name it, those things that happened while I watched, and I cannot speak something that was never in words, speak of things I cannot imagine, could never have seen even as I saw it, and I hide and am grateful for my smell crouched like an animal in that dark hot space.

I shake my head. *Imagine good things*, I say to myself, forefinger pressed firmly between my eyes, *block out the hor-*

ror and imagine good things, I say, but all I can think is that it would be nice to have a hot meal.

I sigh, turn over, and close my eyes, dropping the cigarette into the wet black.

Dawn Is Two Hands Parting
before the Face

Morning arrives in a shout, parting the protective cover of leaves as surely as a hand. I blink and wipe at my eyes furiously. Time is like that here. No gradual change, no softening of the light or gentle graying of night. Instead everything happens rudely, at once: like this war. I stretch carefully so as not to fall out of my perch. My trained eyes scan the terrain, ascertaining very quickly that it is safe. I scramble down. It is a quiet morning, no sound of gunfire, only birdsong and the landscape, the grass flowing like a green mossy carpet from where I stand at the edge of the forest down to the river. But then the war intrudes again: floating past in the river like a macabre regatta is a cluster of corpses. Riding them like barges, and breakfasting at the same time, are a bunch of vultures. I light a cigarette and scratch my belly. Time to move on, maybe catch breakfast on the way. I know to go against the flow of the bodies. They are washing downstream from the killing zone—a town, judging from the number of bodies in the water. I set off.

Life and death are like this river, Grandfather said. You

can go anywhere on its spread as long as you don't try to stop or alter the river's course. But he was wrong. I have cheated death's course many times and I am still here, like an undercurrent, full of a hate dark as any undertow.

A Funnel Is Fingertips
Steepled, Palms Apart

I scan the road ahead and try to figure out what the enemy might have in store for me, if this is their territory now. Ambush is a standard procedure—for both sides. This is how the enemy set their traps: they plant mines in the road verge, in the brush, then they ambush an oncoming troop. The initial volley of fire from them is aimed a little too high so that it kills only a few oncoming soldiers. Naturally, and in spite of the three weeks of boot-camp training and the formations we have been taught to assume, we scatter for cover, stumbling onto the mines, blowing up ourselves and our friends. It is a particularly cruel way to take out an enemy, but since land mines are banned in civilized warfare, the West practically gives them away at cost and in this way they are cheaper than bullets and other arms. If they could, the enemy would have jerry-rigged the mines so they could throw them like grenades, but the firing mechanism of a mine is too sensitive to take such risks. Instead they lay them like a metal undercarpet. When a mine explodes, anyone directly on top will usually be killed. They are lucky. For the rest, shrapnel tears off arms and legs and parts of faces. Mines are like little jumping jacks. You step on one, they arm, you step off, and they jump up about mid-torso high and then explode, ripping you apart. For us, the rebels, mines are as valuable as bullets. We have no generous super-power sugar-daddies and we reuse every mine that we successfully defuse. Waste not want not.

To counter these ambushes, the rebel leaders came up with the funnel. The name reminds me of the white cone my dog wore after he was neutered, and I can hardly make the sign for it without cracking up in soundless mirth. At the tapered end of the funnel, which is the front, are the scouts and mine diffusers. The scouts are split into two groups: the rekies who are strictly there for reconnaissance, and who report directly to the leader and are the only ones with radios or satellite phones; the other group of scouts are called kamikazes. Their job is to draw enemy fire while we mine diffusers get to work clearing the road for the body of the troop, which is spread out in a fan, the two sides ready to flank the enemy if necessary.

My platoon and I are often at the front of every encounter. This has pros and cons. Pros and cons—the language of the invisible manual of John Wayne; invisible or lost. I like lost better—the lost manual of John Wayne. It should probably have a subtitle like my French textbook did: *French Afrique Book One: French Even Africans Can Speak.* Anyway, pros and cons would be a chapter in that manual. John Wayne swore by them.

"Weigh the pros and cons of every situation!" he would shout at us. "It is best to proceed when there are more pros than cons, but not every con is a bad thing. In war we have acceptable losses; provided of course that it is in the service of the greater good . . . It's all in the manual," he would add to forestall Ijeoma's questions.

Thinking about it now, I will pay good money to see that manual. I slap myself. So many digressions—no wonder I have lost my platoon. Pros and cons of being at the front of every battle:

Pros—

• Prime pillaging opportunities.
• The battle is over quicker.
• If you die, it is quick (unless you fall victim to a mine, which can be a slow death sometimes).
• The kamikaze dies first.
• Choice pick of weapons.

The cons?

• Death.
• Death.
• Death.

But regardless of the risks, I will not trade places with the clean-up crew, the platoon of vultures that bring up the rear, whose job is to clean up the dead and ensure the counts are accurate. Some of us have dog tags and some don't, so their job is at best a good guess. I am sure that when the war is over, many of the reported dead will stream back to their families only to be rejected as ghosts or zombies. For us at the front, death is quick, ours and our comrades. For the clean-up crew, death is a lingering disease. Do they get tired of it? Counting the dead is not easy. It is rare to die intact in a war. Bullets and shrapnel from mines and mortars and shells can tear a body to pieces. An arm here, a leg over there in the foliage—all of which have to be retrieved and assembled into the semblance of a complete body before there can be a count. The worst thing about this job may be the irreconcilable math of it: Many of the parts don't add up. This is the enemy's cruelty—that much of the generation who survive this war will not be able to rebuild their communities. Even now it is not uncommon to run across groups of these half-people holding onto life in distant parts of the forest. Even the enemy soldiers spare these pitiful creatures when they come across them.

I remember a group I saw once. Children without arms or legs or both, men with only half a face, women with shrapnel-chewed scars for breasts—all of them holding onto life and hope with a fire that burned feverishly in their eyes. If any light comes from this war, it will come from eyes such as those.

Someone had found a radio and it was tuned to a BBC World Service broadcast of Congolese highlife. There were a bunch of disabled children dancing in a circle. A young girl with one leg standing off to the side leaning on a stick made fun of the dancers. Challenged to do better, she laughed, threw the stick away, and jumped into the circle. She stood still for a moment as though she was getting her bearings, and then she began to move. Still balanced on one leg, her waist began a fierce gyration and her upper body moved the opposite way. Then like a crazy heron, she began to hop around, her waist and torso still shaking. She was an elemental force of nature. I couldn't take my eyes off her. I have never seen anything like it before or since—a small fire sprite shaking the world and reducing grown war-hardened onlookers to tears.

I think of her and the fire I saw burning in the others and I realize the fire burning in me is shame; shame and fear, and it drives me to get up and proceed. I must find my platoon.

Danger Is a Deeper Silence

Time is standing still—literally. My watch, an old Timex that belonged to my father, is fucked. Already broken when he died, it was the only thing of his that my uncle let me inherit. The watch has one of those expanding bracelets made of a metal that was painted gold once, and its face is a mottled brown. Since I've had it, the second and hour hands have fallen off, both nestling like tired armatures in the bottom of the cracked glass case. My life it turns out is a series of minutes. I glance and guess it's about noon now. I have been walking for too long and I am dying of thirst. The river to my right is poisonous with the dead. It would be wise to get off the river road and make my way through the shade of the forest until I can find some water, but the road is faster and I decide to continue on it for now. I look at my broken watch and think, *One more hour.* Rustling the broken arms like pods in a shaker, I head off again.

I have other watches. Nicer watches. Rolex, Patek Philippe, Raymond Weil, Movado—name it. All of them liberated from houses we ransacked or from soldiers who had ransacked other houses before us. And not just watches. I have electronics, cameras, money, jewelry, weapons, shoes, designer clothes, even gold teeth and glasses. Looting is something we all do, rebel and federal troops, officers and enlisted men alike. John Wayne even took a car once, a Lexus that blew up shortly after. That made him angry for a week. We take what we can when we can. Since we have no means of transporting too much for too long, especially as we must keep our weight down for the mines, we made several secret stashes along the way. We figured others might stumble on a cache or two, but with the number we have, we will be well off after the war.

Through it all, my father's watch remains my most treasured possession. That and the medallion of St. Christopher that Ijeoma gave me after she stepped on that mine. She would have taken it off her own neck, except that she no longer had any arms or legs and wasn't much more than a bloody torso, lacerated by shrapnel, body parts scattered in a way that cannot be explained or described. Instead I read her mind, or her eyes, or something, and understood everything—what she wanted, what she regretted—all of it, filling my head like a bad virus. I reach under my shirt and rub the cool metal of the medallion. She said it would protect me for sure now, especially as it had already claimed one victim.

"I am proper sacrifice," she said, and smiled.

I remember it all—every minute of it—vividly. Or at least I remember my memories of it. She lay dying in my arms, and I wiped a tear from her face.

"I'm sorry," I said, not expecting her to answer.

"You disobeyed the rule book," she said.

She was right. I was in the middle of a live minefield assisting a dying comrade, in direct contravention of John Wayne's rules, abandoning my post to help her, endangering myself and the rest of my platoon. But I loved her.

"Don't," I said. "Don't die."

"It's not so bad," she said. "Dying, I mean. It's not so bad."

"Shush," I said.

"Leaving . . ." she began, and then she died. I like to think she was going to say, "Leaving you is hard."

I've often replayed that scene, wishing that I could change some detail. That I had held her back for a quick kiss, thus keeping her from that mine, but being the leader meant having to act a little indifferent toward her in front of the others. If she resented the change, she said nothing. I squeeze my eyes tightly closed, but her mocking smile can't be shut out.

Voices, and not imaginary ones, are coming down the road from a hidden bend. I don't hesitate, loping across the short grass between me and the forest, gaining cover quickly. There is no point in waiting around to find out if they are friend or foe. I need to get to a town and get some food and drink, so I plunge deeper into the forest, moving fast if not silently through the undergrowth. At this point, silence doesn't matter anymore. Even if they hear me, they will imagine it is some animal. I press on until I break through the cover into a circular natural clearing in the forest. It has been widened and I can tell from the cut shrubbery where nature stopped and machetes moved forward. There are a couple of open and empty metal shipping containers, a few bombed-out vehicles, including an ambulance and a ruined armored car. Something about the ambulance fills me with a nostalgia that makes my eyes water from the sweetness of it. I stop and scan the clearing. Apart from a few crows, the place is abandoned. Something about it is very familiar though and I realize I have been here before. The entire platoon has been here. Just before Ijeoma got blown up, after the church incident, after I shot John Wayne. There is no mistaking the statues the guys liberated from the church— the wooden Jesus in a peeling red tunic with one leg missing where Nebu had chopped it off the day we killed a monkey and needed firewood to cook; Jesus' leg was the only dry wood anywhere on that rainy day, the rain had made it possible to catch the monkey as it slipped on a wet branch. I couldn't eat it because it reminded me too much of the dead child in my dreams, and of that night we stumbled on that gory feast, those gorgons, and I left the campsite as the others cooked and ate it. Later, Ijeoma brought me an open tin of Spam from a box we'd liberated from some rich man's house.

I look around, eyes meeting those of the sad-looking Virgin whose white-painted concrete body has turned green from rain. She is mottled from the bullet holes we inflicted with target practice. I approach slowly. I am on the right track, this much is sure. It seems I am retracing my steps through places we passed. Something is off about it though, and yet as much as it is nagging at me, I cannot pinpoint what it is exactly, but I know it has something to do with the chronology of my memories. The time between them is shrinking, I think. If I didn't still have this damn concussion I might be able to figure it out.

I approach the containers. Buried under them in a metal box is a cache of food we left here. It is probably bad, but it's worth trying. Like a chicken, I scratch in the dirt under it until I pull out the metal box that used to house the rounds for the M60 machine gun we had mounted on the roof of the bombed-out truck. There are several tins of food and I quickly drive my knife through the top of one lid into the soft meat inside. Even as I do it I think it is stupid that I didn't check to see if the contents were booby-trapped. If the cache had been disturbed it would be impossible to tell because the ground was old.

There is no booby-trap, no explosion, just the sweet taste of stale sardines in olive oil filling my mouth, my knife still embedded in the smile of the woman on the tin. *Queen of the Coast*, it says.

I have happy memories about this place. We spent a long time here, hiding out from the war, being teenagers, and in that forest idyll, the change the war had wrought on us seemed very subtle. When we first stumbled on this oasis, the rain had collected in a seasonal pond and we lived in the burned-out trucks and armored vehicles, feeding on the forest's grace and swimming in the pond. Ijeoma and I lived as a couple in the back of the old ambulance, making love with desperation tinged with the foreknowledge of loss. If we could have, we would have waited out the war here. We didn't want to move on, didn't want to press on to the front. We weren't stupid and we were certainly no longer idealistic. We only moved forward when we were forced to. It was the systematic strafing campaign aimed at flushing out rebel soldiers hiding in the forest, a campaign that rained bombs on us, turning the forest into an inferno that made us leave. When we headed off, it was in the direction I have just come from.

I look around a little confused that there is no evidence of the bombing. The forest is lush and green. Is it possible that it grew back so fully so quickly? Things are off and I can't quite place why. It's like having something stuck in my teeth just out of reach of my tongue: irritating. What's the use of hurrying things; it will come when it comes. I have other things to worry about, things more concrete.

I fall asleep under the truck I've been digging by, while all around a gentle rain falls, and I don't dream of the child's head; in the distance heavy artillery fire approaches. But for now I sleep.

Full of fish.

Love Is a Backhanded Stroke
to the Cheek

It is a curious experience—to be inside your dream and outside it, lucid and yet sleeping deeply. But in this war so much has happened to make even this seem normal. I dream of Ijeoma and the night I lost my virginity to her. It is true that I had already had sex by then: John Wayne had forced me to rape someone, but that didn't count. That was sex, rape, this was love; this was choice.

I cannot even tell if this is how it happened or whether my dream is some kind of wish fulfillment. It is the same day John Wayne forced me to rape that woman, and afterwards, while the others gather around a fire to roast a goat, Ijeoma takes me to the river. It is dark down here and I can barely make out her face. She makes me sit by the water and she washes my feet and my face, then she strips off and dives into the water. I watch her move through the dark fluid like it is a second skin. My breath catches in my throat, way back, so it is hard to breathe.

"Come in," she calls.

I am scared of the dark water and cannot. I know I will

die if I get in, but my fear is so irrational I don't even speak it. I just shake my head.

"Coward," she says, splashing me.

I laugh and get up. I strip as though I am about to get in the water but I don't. I sit back down on the dew-damp grass and feel it tickle my skin. This is sensual yet childlike, free and unconcerned. While I don't feel innocent, and even though I no longer know what that can mean, it seems attainable. Suddenly Ijeoma is standing over me and I look up. In the faint light I see her body—the womanly swell of her hips belying the small buds on her chest. Her skin is wrinkled from the cold water and she is dripping water onto me, each drop falling slowly and with a touch that burns, but I cannot wait for the next drop. She kneels and kisses me. I close my eyes and lose myself in the damp moment. Later, we are dressing and she turns smiling and says: "You should stop fighting now."

I don't know what it means. I want to ask her but I can feel myself waking up.

Listening Is a Hand Cupping an Ear like a Seashell

Daylight comes like rust corroding night. It is cool from last night's rain and I stretch slowly, rested for the first time in months. I roll out from under the truck and walk the perimeter of the old camp, peeing as I go, stopping only to scratch my balls. Returning to the truck I slept under, I fish out a can of beans, bayonet it open, and spoon it cold with the tip of my knife. I have to move on. If the voices I just heard are enemy soldiers, they will soon be here.

I search through the cabs and backs of the trucks for any kind of bag. It seems like a good idea to pack some food for the road—and maybe some loot that I can trade for favors. There is nothing. I leave the armored vehicles for last, afraid to jump into their dark bellies. I feel like the pygmy on the elephant hunt who has to cut into the beast and push past organs to cut out its heart, thereby declaring it an open feast.

Not that I have ever seen a pygmy or even an elephant, except at the zoo before the war. I must have heard it somewhere, maybe I saw it in a documentary in school. Absently I wonder whether the animals in the zoo have been eaten in the food shortages. The thought of lions and giraffes clubbed to death for meat upsets me. If Ijeoma were here, she would say my feelings are irrational. She would say I am just homesick.

"It's not the animals you mourn," she would say. "It is your home."

The voice in my head is loud enough to make me look around, half expecting to see her. Apart from the toads I can hear in the muddy bottom of the near empty pond, I am alone.

Plucking up courage, I jump inside the first armored car and root around. Nothing. Gaining the light again, I sit on top and smoke a cigarette. There on the barrel of the gun is a bright red knit bag. How could I have missed it? I smoke and watch it for a while, almost as if it is a mirage.

When I was a boy, my mother taught me how to crochet. I loved it. The way one knot would slip into another and another until the thread spread into a wide but strong web, while the steel crocked needle, like a shepherd's stave, flashed. I used to imagine I was God, and the doily or cap I was knitting was a world, and the flash of the needle was lightning doing my bidding, spreading life like a primal shiver of fire.

My father was alive then and he didn't mind. He saw it as a harmless distraction, one that in fact presented the opportunity of a metaphor for him teaching me the Koran, the suras learned stitch by stitch—*there is no God but Allah*; hook and stitch; *and Mohammed is his true prophet*; circle with the wool; *blessings be upon his name;* pull needle through and loop. He was a gentle man, my father the imam. But my uncle, the distant relative who arrived when my father died and claimed my mother as his wife in the name of some old custom, hated me and he hated that I didn't play the rough games like other boys. He beat me so bad; and my mother watched, afraid or unable to help, I wasn't sure why, but I hated her for it. Why would she let this goat possess her? One day she showed me the crawl space in the ceiling, and I would hide up there for hours crocheting, wrapped around the wooden beams, building one huge web that became a hammock, became a shelter.

Tossing the cigarette, I jump down, grab the bag, and stuff it full of tins of food, all well past their sell-by dates. I also stuff in cartons of cigarettes, some cheap plastic lighters, some watches, and a few notes of nearly worthless local money—they will make good bribes. I pick up the bag, my gun, and stuff my feet into a pair of old boots, before heading off in the direction of the road.

I crouch in the grass by the roadside for a long time watching a roadblock up ahead. Hidden in a curve of the road, it is hard to see what is beyond and in fact who is manning it, and how many. It is clearly unwise to proceed so I decide to use the river. Darting across the road, I drop noiselessly into the water. I need to head upriver, in the direction of the roadblock, because I know beyond it is a town and I might find shelter, but there is no way of getting past the roadblock unseen. Or even of getting across the river to flank it along the other bank. There is also the matter of the boat I saw the other night. If it comes back while I am still visible, it will be the end of me and I can kiss any chance of reuniting with my platoon goodbye. The safest thing to do is to grab hold of one of the corpses, get under it, and float downstream for a while. If I can circle back to the mangroves, I might be able to find an adjacent tributary and use it to make my way back up, closer to the other bank.

The smell is beyond anything I even have words for. I close my eyes and throw up soundlessly into the water as I float along. Time, in the water, loses all weight and the day passes slowly. Finally, when I think I can no longer ride the cadaver, when I think the smell of death will overwhelm me, when I think it might be better to die than to carry these new memories into life, I feel land under my feet and realize that my macabre craft is being washed ashore onto a sandbank. Still cautious, I push my head up, hand cupped around my ear as though to catch more sound, and listen: for the boat; for people; for danger. Satisfied, I stumble onto the island. In the dim light I can make out the shapes of some huts. This was obviously one of those temporary shelters that fishermen used, like hunters used hunting lodges, to fish out of, smoke their catch, and then head home in the rainy season when the sandbanks were swallowed by the quick-rising water.

I make my way into one and crawl up into the rafters to keep safe from crocodiles and fall asleep. I dream the moon is the child's head smiling at me.

Fish Is a Hand Swimming
through the Air

I don't know how long I've been stranded on the sandbank, having lost track of time. Night blends into day blends into night, seamlessly. The sound of distant gunfire reaches me though I feel no need to return to the war. I have lost my taste for death. But I do want to find my platoon. I am a little concerned that it is taking this long to catch up with them. I calculate that I was probably unconscious for a few hours, so they can't be that far ahead. Of course I have been traveling alone which has meant doubling back and now spending time on this isle. I have probably lost days now, but I am a skilled tracker and should be able to catch them still. I have to get off this shifting island first; but something is keeping me here.

Life on the sandbank isn't bad. I have repaired one of the huts reasonably, and my diet of fish is supplemented by a small garden left by one of the fishermen. It has some yams, tomatoes, peppers, and even vegetables. It won't last much longer though, but for now, like Robinson Crusoe, I am content not to make any plans. Luckily there are several earthenware pots full of rainwater which tastes cool and refreshing, if mildly of earth. Yet even if it tasted brackish, I am glad for it. Drinking the river water, with all the rotting corpses it holds, will surely kill me.

I sleep in some planks I have rigged up in the rafters. On the ground I would be too vulnerable to the crocodiles that now come boldly onto the sandbank believing it deserted. A few well-placed shots might scare them off, but I am loathe to waste ammo.

Though I still don't rest, I sleep a lot now. There isn't much else to do. Long deep nights where my dreams are treks across star-spangled deserts with my dead comrades and relatives calling in the distance just out of reach. Always out of reach. Lazy siestas, the sun tickling me through the holes in the thatch, weevils causing dust to fall, waking me up sneezing. But even in daylight, even in these siestas, I am plagued by vivid nightmares. I always wake up sweating, the dreams leaving a tangy bitter aftertaste for hours.

I stretch and head for the water, distracting myself by trying to fish without a line, dribbling a string of saliva into the water like Grandfather taught me. I have been trying it for days without much luck, but today feels different. The string of saliva sets up gentle ripples and bubbles in the water not unlike those caused by a fish. Soon the catfish beneath me slows to a halt, whiskers reading the water for the intruder. Half hypnotized, it just floats there, senses deflected from the shadows above. My hand snakes out with the speed of a cobra and catches the fat catfish behind its head. I pull it out and slam it on the bank once.

It dies.

The Soul Has No Sign

I build a fire and slowly roast the fish. I love the smell—the dry crackle of its oil dribbling into the fire, its scent of mud and something else. It reminds me of home, of warm gari soaking in sea-salted water and the damp funk of the Cross River sweating against its banks.

When it is cooked, I eat slowly, the flesh exploding in fluffy pink clouds that taste wistfully of smoke. Every time I eat fish, I remember Grandfather's story of the lake in the middle of the world and the fish that live there. I can hear his voice in my head now. I can see clearly the night he told me.

There is a lake in the middle of the world.

Grandfather said.

This is the oldest truth of our people. This is the oldest lie.

A lake of fire and water. This lake is a legend of the Igbo. It is invisible, hidden in a fold in time, but there.

That day we were fishing on the Cross: a breathtaking river over two miles wide, in many places etched out of the horizon only by the line of palm trees on the opposite bank.

It was dotted with sandbanks—many of them a good acre big. These glistening white mounds humped the river every dry season and lasted months, developing a whole ecosystem of water hyacinths, bull rushes, fluorescent white egrets, basking hippos or crocodiles, and fishermen camps.

There are many tales about how the Cross got its name. There are always many tales here, Grandfather said. Don't trust any of them, he always cautioned. Trust all of them, he warned. Some say it got its name because the Igbos are Hebrews who wandered down to West Africa from Judea and some of them brought fragments of Christ's Cross with them. Some say it is because in the past the Igbo used to crucify thieves and murderers on its bank. Some say it was named after the frustrated British engineer who worked for the Colonial Service Works Department. Not that he was named Cross. Just that he refused to make sacrifices to placate the water spirits, so the mother of them, the mami-wata, pushed down every bridge the man tried to build across it to link the first colonial capital of Calabar with the hinterlands. This was long before the capital was moved to Lagos, which I guess had friendlier spirits.

Eight bridges this unnamed British engineer tried to build, until in frustration he threw down his T-slide and retired to Sussex muttering about "bloody nigger river can't be crossed, I won't let it become my cross." But it did. He carried it around Sussex until mami-wata came for him on his deathbed, or so I imagine. Still, the Cross flowed: a magnificent river.

Canoes; some no bigger than single-person kayaks, others bordering on small schooners and ships, glided up and down the river, skating like dragonflies, propelled by the powerful pull of oars or poles exerted by knotted biceps.

That was a special night: the gentle slap of the water on wood, the rustle of drying salt, the calls of river birds, the strange hippo barks, and the ticklish smell of the herbs burning gently to drive away mosquitoes wove magic around my senses.

I trailed my fingers in the water, sifting as if for a morsel of archaic wisdom carried by the river's memory. Grandfather said this river was older than Job.

"In the Bible?" I asked.

"Yes," he said, smiling.

He said when the earth was young and this land still a dream, the river cut its path through a mountain, a tear of sweat racing down a giant's face.

"How do you know?"

"Because it speaks to me. Hush, listen."

I couldn't hear anything.

Neither of us paid much attention as we drifted down the delta to the mouth of the sea. I must have fallen asleep, fingers still trawling the water for wisdom, because I woke to the dry rasp of a tongue on my fingers. Startled and unsure what creature it was, I drew my fingers back with a yelp. A dolphin clicked at me in laughter, dousing me with salty water as though in benediction, and vanished in a white spray for the ocean.

"Lucky boy. What a blessing," Grandfather said. "That dolphin has just taken your soul for safekeeping—always."

"My soul? Does that mean I will never die?"

"Maybe."

That was when he told me about the sacred lake with the pillar, half-water, half-fire, all woman.

"We believe we were the first sentient beings in the universe. Our father, Amadioha, sent a bolt of lightning down to strike a silk cotton tree and the tree split open revealing man and woman. But after Amadioha made men, they ran wild with the lust of power in their noses. Who knows why? Maybe Amadioha wasn't skilled in making people, all his manifestations seem as though made by a mid-tier elemental. So, God, not Amadioha, sent down its essence. It descended as a pillar: half-fire, half-water. It descended to and arose from the surface of a dark lake in the center of the earth. This new deity we call Idemilli. To control our excess and ensure our evolution, Idemilli took all the power from men. Now, to enter into the confines of power we have to be deemed worthy enough by the guardian."

"And what does this guardian look like?"

"She is a woman all fire and water and more brilliant than a thousand suns; at least those who have been lucky to see her say so."

"Why is she a woman?"

"Because she has to be."

"Tell me more about the lake. Does it still exist?"

"Some say it always has, in some dimensional warp."

"Have you ever seen it?"

"Even if I had, you wouldn't believe me and I wouldn't tell you."

"Does everyone know about the lake?" I asked.

"No."

"Is it sacred?"

"Very. It is the repository of human souls who are yet to gain access into the world: a source of great power for any dibia who enters there. Legend says that the fish in the lake guard the souls, swallowed deep in their bellies."

"Why the fish?"

"Because the ancestors are concerned with the living, angels with the running of the universe, and neither elementals nor men can be trusted."

"And this lake is real?"

"Very."

"But it sounds like a tall tale."

"It is."

"I don't understand."

"Nobody does. Everybody does. It is real because it is a tall tale. This lake is the heart of our people. This lake is love. If you find it, and find the pillar, you can climb it into the very heart of God," he said.

"Where is this lake, Grandfather?"

He tapped me on the breastbone.

"Here. It is at the center of you, because you are the world."

"How will I find it?"

He taught me a song. We sang it over and over, together, for the rest of the night until I couldn't tell where his voice ended and mine began, and where mine ended and the river began and where the river ended and my blood began.

But I have forgotten that song. I wish I hadn't because I think it would bring me much comfort to sing it. *Oh well*, I think, eating the last of the fish, wondering whose soul I can taste smoking down to my stomach, and if anyone has eaten mine yet.

Ghosts Are a Gentle Breath
over Moving Fingers

Whatever I am dreaming about wakes me dripping with sweat. Judging from the light, it is midafternoon. I jump down and walk outside, surveying the banks to make sure there are no basking crocodiles. The bank is clear, but I can't be sure of the water, so I throw some fish I caught earlier into different parts of the river, watching closely for any ripple that would indicate the presence of the water leopards. Everything is perfectly still. Placing my rifle on the edge of the bank, I dive in. The water is tepid. Not too different from the temperature outside. I swim for a while, trying to wash the stale sweat off, and the bad dreams with it: difficult without soap. Noticing what looks like a log floating past, I race for the sandbank. Better safe.

I dry slowly in the dying embers of the sun, and as the water evaporates a slight chill wrinkles my skin. For some reason, I feel like I am being kept here on the sandbank by some spirit's still unfulfilled wish. It is a stupid superstition but something I feel strongly nonetheless, despite the fact that there has been no proof of it. An egret lands nearby and studies me with curious eyes. I feel a breeze across the river's face and look up. A canoe drifts slowly past, a skeleton piloting it. I shiver, suppressing an urge to scream. Sometimes my childishness still plagues me.

The canoe becomes entangled in some lilies growing in a green and white cluster, and though the tides are pulling at it, I know because the lilies are nodding their white heads in time that the boat will not dislodge. The skeleton sways back and forth with the boat's motion and it makes me think of an elaborate decoration on a Swiss clock. There is a cobweb between the bony arm and the empty chest. It is beautiful and shimmers in the fading light. I wonder how long this poor soul has been lost, even as I admire the cobweb, thinking it reminds me of another time. Of the doilies and small caps I used to crochet all those years ago.

I reach out my hand and try to touch the spider's web. It is perfect. But I can't reach it. *Just as well*, I think, catching myself. For all I know, this could be a booby trap. The enemy knows our reverence for death and its ritual and could have just sent this downriver intentionally. I examine the bones. There is no way to know what he, or she, died of. Standing up, I back away from the boat and gather some pebbles of varying size and weight and then lob them at the canoe. If it were booby-trapped, this would set off any bombs. Satisfied that it is clean, I walk over to one of the huts and pull a long pole from its roof, and with great difficulty I maneuver the canoe aground.

Leaving it for a while, I dig a shallow grave in the shifting sand, knowing it will be washed away in next year's flood. But that is unimportant. What is important is that this person be buried. Be mourned. Be remembered. Even for a minute. Before I take the skeleton out of the canoe, I reach in and pull the cobweb gently free. I drape it over my head like a cap and then lift the skeleton with ease, careful not to shake any bones loose. To come back complete, it is important that one leave complete. Laying it in the grave, I cover it hurriedly and say a soft prayer and play "Taps" on my harmonica. It is the least I can do.

There are so many restless spirits here. Maybe this is why I am dallying here, delayed by the need of this lonely spirit to find rest. Tomorrow I will leave with the salvaged canoe. That is the way here. I feel the grateful blessing of the spirit in the wind on my cheek.

"Farewell, friend," I whisper.

Truth Is Forefinger to Tongue Raised Skyward

Every star is a soul, every soul is a destiny meant to be lived out. They fill the night sky, revealing like a diviner's spread the destiny of those gifted in reading their drift, their endless shift, like a desert, revealing and burying the way alternately.

I have killed many people during the last three years. Half of those were innocent, half of those were unarmed— and some of those killings have been a pleasure. But even with all this, even with the knowledge that there are some sins too big for even God to forgive, every night my sky is still full of stars; a wonderful song for night.

I sigh and lean back in the canoe. The current has changed direction and is flowing upriver now; inland. The corpses, like a reluctant company of dancers, bump into each other as they hit the sudden swerve of the water, bump into each other and waltz lazily back the way they came. The corpses seem to be mocking me. They seem to say, *Don't worry, you'll be one of us soon, you'll join us in this slow dance.*

My Luck is dead.

This is what my mother would say if I die in this war. I

say *would* because she is already dead; but that is another matter. My Luck: that's what she named me, fourth son after three daughters, all of whom died of mysterious sicknesses before they were eight. In this culture, a woman who bears only daughters is not worth much to her husband and family: maybe not worth anything. In my family, the women lose a lot of babies. Like Aunt Gladys. I remember the night she came round to our house all bruised up from a beating from her husband. I was only five but I remember it. We were all sitting by the fire outside roasting corn and pears, my father, my mother, and I.

They talked in muted whispers, my parents and her, in the low glow from the fire, with the shadows riding close by; they looked haunted. Though they were whispering, I could make out that she had somehow lost her baby, and I thought it was careless of Aunt Gladys to lose her baby like that. I mean how can it be in your stomach one minute then lost the next, sailing down a river of red. The last part I had just heard: Aunt Gladys saying it was like a river of red, the blood that gushed from her. It made me think of the chicken we had killed for our Sunday dinner that still had unlaid eggs in her. My father took the eggs out, his eyes sad. I poked them, surprised to find that they were soft like snake eggs, and my stick pierced the soft case of one and the egg burst, revealing a spit of blood and mashed bones and feathers. Father covered it in sand and muttered under his breath.

"What are you doing?" I asked.

"Praying. You should too."

But I didn't. I still haven't: not for any of the lives I have taken. Or the ones I have lost. But it was hard to imagine Aunt Gladys's river of red having small crushed bones and feathers. Does her husband pray even now for the life he took? I was very quiet, even then I said very little. I should have been asleep and it was a rare privilege to be allowed to sit with the grown-ups, so I wasn't about to mess that up by talking. I looked up from the ground and studied Aunt Gladys crying there and risking everything, then I stood up and came over and curled myself into the small of her back, my tiny arms around her belly. I'll never forget the sigh she let out. It was like she had taken the last breath of air on the planet but had to let it go.

"My Luck," she said. "My Luck, do you know what lonely feels like?"

I didn't know. To my five-year-old mind it might have been like losing my puppy or the dirty secondhand teddy I loved so much.

"No, Aunty," I said.

"Lonely is a cold, itchy back," she said.

I laughed and snuggled closer, one hand scratching her back through her thin blouse. She sighed happily and my parents laughed. I keep that night close, like a well-worn photograph of family, of a time when we were happy. My father died shortly after that night, and my uncle, my father's half-brother, became my father and my mother became his mistress, and I the burden that stared at him daily with a malevolence he couldn't beat out of me.

I stretch and lean further back and stare into night, the wood of the canoe hard against my back like a hand. A little fire burns in the leaking metal pail I found on the sandbank. I filled it with hot coals and kindling and set it in a wet block of wood in the center of the canoe; the way I had seen Grandfather do so many times. It would keep me warm this cold night, and the light, too faint to be seen from the bank, was enough to comfort me in that river of the dead. Fire and starlight and the wood of the boat; and something else— hope that I will find home in the morning. Thinking of Aunt Gladys, I know now of course that she was right. The heart is not where we feel loneliness. It is in the back. I press mine harder against the wood behind me, but it is cold and wet from the river. With drooping eyes I watch the fire die.

Mercy Is a Palm Turning
Out from the Heart

This woman's eyes are cold and hard and dark like onyx and I wake straight into that gaze. One that reveals nothing and flinches from nothing; if I am death, she is ready. If I mean no harm, she will ignore me; I hope. My gesture is one of supplication and if she understands it, she doesn't show it. Her gaze takes in my torn clothes, my haggard face, and the gun, and also the scapular that has come loose. I can't make out what she is thinking.

I hesitate, letting her gaze wander over me as I scan the bank for any signs of other people. She appears to be alone. I return my eyes to her and search her for weapons. All she has is a long pole with a makeshift metal hook on the end. A bag stands by her feet and I see it is filling up with loot. Rings, watches, compacts, a handbag, some good shoes, jewelry, and with a shudder I realize what she is doing, or was doing before she happened upon me. She uses the hook to pull bodies onto the shore and robs them of their valuables. It is despicable what she is doing, I think, and wonder if I drifted into the bank or whether she pulled the canoe in with the intent of robbing me. Ghoul. At least when I rob, I rob the living, I think, feeling superior to her. But if she is ashamed by her profession, nothing in her face reveals it.

It is a bright day and my broken watch reveals nothing about the time. I can only guess it is about midday. I thank whatever gods or goddesses watched over me while I slept. There is a road behind the woman and I can't tell if this is the one from yesterday or if I have drifted back to the bank with the roadblock. Nothing looks familiar.

The woman gives me one final look, makes the sign of the cross, and goes back to fishing for corpses as though she has dismissed me, as though with that token sign she has somehow rendered me invisible.

"Mother, where am I?" I try to signal, using the generic term for respect. But either she can't see me anymore, doesn't understand, or doesn't want to. I get out of the canoe and walk toward her. She pauses and turns to look at me; the sun is directly in my face and I am squinting. She hesitates, then spits, almost shouting, "Tufia!" the old word for banishing spirits or bad things. I smile and something in my face softens her, and for a minute her eyes are pure tenderness and the look unsettles me, brings back memories of the first woman I raped, a woman her age, and I stumble back confused, wondering if she is real or if she is a ghost, an apparition drawn by the river goddess mami-wata from my guilt; to punish me. As I stagger back from her, my mind staggers back in time, but fragments are all I stumble over.

John Wayne was yelling at me. There were villagers run-

ning in panic. There were houses and huts burning. Also gra-
naries. Bullets from indiscriminate guns cut down plants,
animals, and people. The platoon was screaming. Ijeoma, the
only girl among the attackers, stood to one side, watching,
too afraid perhaps to cry. But something moved behind her
eyes. John Wayne and I were standing in a room. A woman
huddled under the bed. *Why do they do that?* I thought.
Hiding under a bed never saved anyone. John Wayne pulled
her out and threw her on the bed. Ripping her clothes off,
he ordered me to rape her. I hesitated.

"You are the only one who hasn't raped anyone yet!" he
barked at me.

I wanted to ask him what this skirmish, this fight, this
destruction of an innocent village had to do with our mission
to defuse mines, but I knew better. I looked at the woman.
My hesitation puzzled her and she stopped crying. John
Wayne was angry at my insubordination and he pointed his
gun at my head.

"Rape or die," he said, and I knew he meant it. As I
dropped my pants and climbed onto the woman, I won-
dered how it was that I had an erection. Some part of me was
enjoying it and that perhaps hurt me the most. I entered the
woman and strangely she smiled. I moved, and as much as I
wanted to pretend, I couldn't lie, I enjoyed it. The woman's
eyes were tender, as if all she saw was a boy lost. She stroked
my hair tenderly, whispering as I sobbed: "It's all right son,
it's all right. Better the ones like you live." When I came,
John Wayne laughed and put two rounds into the woman's

head, spraying my face with her blood. The woman died with that look of absolute tenderness in her eyes.

Ijeoma found me. She knew, but she had too much grace to say anything. That night, in the rubble of that village, while the others roasted a goat, she washed the blood from my face.

"You have the taste now," she said.

I nodded. I knew what she meant. I was thirteen, armed and lost in a war with the taste for rape.

"I will save you," she said.

And she did. She became my girlfriend and that night and every night after that, whenever we raided a town or a village, while the others were raping the women and sometimes the men, Ijeoma and I made desperate love, crying as we came, but we did it to make sure that amongst all that horror, there was still love. That it wouldn't die here, in this place.

I return to the moment of that woman's look and the look this woman is giving me here at the riverbank. I turn from her and run through the thick patch of tall grass on the bank, across the road, and make for the forest. I can still feel her eyes on me. I decide to rest and move closer to the town that must be nearby under the cover of darkness.

I climb a tree and doze.

Dreaming Is Hands Held
in Prayer over the Nose

Maybe this is true. That there are some of us who give love and some of us who take love; and that those who give can't help giving just as those who take can't help taking; and maybe this is what holds the world in balance.

I dream my hate comes back and she is a woman made of night dancing in the middle of a lake I have seen only in Grandfather's stories and she has claws of fire and breath of ice and her laughter, as she turns in dance, is a band tight as a vice across my heart choking life from it, and as I am gasping for breath all I can think is, *What a thing of beauty she is, what a thing.* Then a light breaks in the east, over the lake, and approaches, an orb smaller than a star but no less bright. I see it is Ijeoma and she opens her arms and the woman made of my hate fills her, slowly extinguishing her light, and she falls from the sky, and as she falls, her light fading, the band around my chest loosens and I see her smile so sadly yet so full of love.

I wake to darkness. Breathing heavily I fumble for a cigarette and stick one in my mouth. In a fleeting kind of way,

I wonder how come this pack never seems to run out, but then a deeper thought takes hold.

I need to find that town and my platoon.

I want to say a prayer for Ijeoma, but I feel silly. It is only a dream. I shake it off and head back to the road. In the dark it looks like it might lead to the underworld.

Shit.

Town Is Hands Making Boxes in the Air

A minnow skirting through weeds in a pool, a plane skims trees that ripple like a dense Afro. I pause and listen. From the engine pitch I can tell it isn't a bomber, probably a Red Cross or reconnaissance plane. Down the dark road, in the distance, the lights of a town beckon and I follow.

The market, built around a central square, is alive even this late. People move back and forth. Night markets are a common feature of this war—there is no nighttime bombing or strafing. I stop by a telephone booth, gleaming white and chrome. It is growing out of a pile of baskets that houses angry chickens. There is no receiver and it most likely hasn't worked since the war started. An interloper, it is regarded suspiciously by the sheep grazing on the rubbish spewed by the market: tin cans, paper, cellophane, fruit peels, rotten yams. The road across the market is a dirt track, mined with potholes. As I make my way through the throng of people shopping, or looking to steal, scents chase after me: goats, chickens, open sewers, muddy earth, dry thatch, rotting fruit, and vegetables.

I leave the market, crossing a small bridge humping a

tired stream. Under a mango tree, in the deeper shadows, cows drink from the belly of a canoe sailing on a pile of sand. Everywhere, madmen and mendicants call. Children: bulbous heads pendulous over hunger-distended bellies with eyes washed out like the earth here. I stop in front of a flaking, dusty building. Somewhere inside, a generator hacks in coughy spurts and the lights flicker in sympathy. A worn sign announces: *Die Hard Motel and Eatery.* I make to enter, but lying across the threshold, dry, brown, dead, and molting, is a lizard. I hesitate. Lizards are sometimes seen as symbols of rebirth, but every rebirth requires a death. I hover on the porch and an old man hunched in the corner sees the lizard and me, and smiling says: "Faith is not a gift. It is earned."

I don't know what he means, so I ignore him.

He spits into the night: "Tufia! Even the dead ignore me!"

Shellshock, I think, and return my attention to the interior of the bar. Several rebel soldiers, officers, I think, are eating at a table near the door, although they seem to be doing more drinking than eating right now. I stare at the plates of rice and stewed meat on the table and feel my stomach knot and my mouth water. Judging by the number of bottles strewn about the place, the men are drunk. One of them is telling a joke so loudly I can hear it out here.

"There are three construction workers, one of them is Igbo, one is Yoruba, and the other Hausa . . ." At this he spits.

"Enemy!" one soldier slurs, interrupting.

"Shut up, I'm talking! Anyway, the Igbo man opens his lunch pack and says, 'Oh no! Not rice again. If I get one more rice dinner, I will throw myself off this scaffolding.' The same is repeated by the Yoruba and Hausa man, except that the food in question is beans and okra respectively. The next day they all get together for lunch. The Igbo man sees his lunch. It is rice. He throws himself from the scaffolding and dies. The Yoruba man sees his is beans and throws himself after the Igbo man. The Hausa man soon follows." The soldier pauses to take a drink from his glass, puts it down, and regardless of the fact that his comrades are half asleep, he continues. "At the inquest, the Igbo man's wife says she had no idea he didn't like rice and she would have changed his lunch if she knew. The Yoruba man's wife says the same. The Hausa man's wife is completely confused. 'I don't understand why he killed himself,' she says. 'For the past twenty years, Hassan has been making his own lunch.'"

Ever since the troubles, and the war, several racist jokes about the enemy have been circulating. This was one of the more famous ones. It is funny, but nonetheless I am tired of all this hate. The joke reminds me of my life in the north before the war.

The call to prayer cracked the skin of sleep. Starting softly, the muezzin's voice trembled and then the chant grew robust. As the muezzin's voice ruffled its feathers and strutted, the call rose to a single point. One note screaming in adoration of the most high. It trembled there in the sunshine for a few minutes before cutting off abruptly. There was a pause, a silence that itself was a call, a prayer. Then the muezzin's voice began the call again. Softly, it built to a crescendo, then died again on that abrupt point, dropping the faithful into the pit of belief. Every morning the call came, rousing me. For the faithful it was joy, while the infidels fought it, struggling to wrap sleep tighter around the senses, but for me it was the voice of my father the imam. When the call ended, its last note a silent scream to Allah, the compound came awake.

It is a terrible thing in this divided nation, even in its infancy, for an Igbo man to be Muslim. I will never know why my father chose that path; one that put him outside his own community, his own people, most of whom are Catholic, and made him a thing that the people who would later become our enemies feared: a hybrid. Even though he had been a Muslim since he was fifteen and traveling as a singer with a band, and an imam for twenty, the only mosque they gave him was inside Sabon Gari: the foreigners' ghetto. Everyone hated the mosque, sitting as it did by decree of the Saraduana in the midst of the Christian enclave. Everyone hated my father. Yet he was the one they came to for arbitration, for help, to borrow money, and to circumcise their sons. For a long time I hated my father too, but since he died, I have been trying to love him.

I look in at the soldiers and realize that somewhere along the line, somewhere in this war, I have lost my appetite for it. I want nothing more than to return to the safety of my platoon and to outlive this madness. I am tired. I sink onto the floor of the porch, not too far from the old man who spoke earlier, and I wonder if he just grew tired too. I light a cigarette, turning to offer one to the old man. He takes it greedily and lights up from the match I hold out to him. The price of coming this far has been too much. From my hiding space in the ceiling to this porch, there has been nothing but blood since the night my mother died. I didn't come down for days after.

It was hot up there, the zinc roof heating up quickly in the sun, my hiding place soon becoming an oven, and I had to strip naked and sip continuously on the water my mother smuggled up. The roof was peppered with rust holes and the sun dripped through in rivers of hot oil, mixing the shouts of the marauding mobs outside, the scent of death, burning flesh, and the screams of the dying into a fire that burned me, patterning my psyche in polka dots of fear.

Finally, I unfurled my body from its cramped position. For the past two weeks there had been pogroms against the Igbos, a frenzy of murder and looting, and the streets were littered with so many bodies. Anyone who had even the slightest resemblance to the Bantu Igbo was killed. The litmus test for those in the shadowlands between was the ability to recite obscure sura from the Koran, or the taking of a life identified as Igbo. The night I left, I stood in the backyard of the tenement, which was enclosed by the U-shaped building. One wing housed the kitchens and bathrooms, the other L the two-room flats that housed the eight families.

Before the troubles, the yard echoed with life: children playing in giggling starts, mothers shouting gossip at each other, men sitting on benches playing checkers and drinking beer, music spilling out of rooms mixing with smells from the kitchens, giving the courtyard extra spice. I remembered the games of cricket, and Paul, who could bowl so fast his main job in the rebel army, if he is still alive, must be lobbing grenades instead of curve balls.

It was deserted. Most of the neighbors were dead or had fled south to safety. Something was rattling in the empty kitchens; some hungry rat despairing. Cobwebs hung in fine lacy decay from the soot-blackened walls. The bathrooms stood still in bracken-scum-surfaced puddles. A lovely breeze blew a newspaper across the courtyard vainly fluttering against the silence.

Hidden in a small latch space behind the headboard of my parents' bed, I found the rolled-up bundle of knives. I took them out. One of my chores was cleaning and honing those knives: the imam's circumcision knives. Small, curved blades that could cut through flesh with a whisper of effort. I grew to love them, polishing the silver blades until they shone. I stroked them, played with them, spoke to them. They in turn spoke of the blood-spattered hysteria of the younger boys and the grim, tight-lipped grunting and moaning of the older boys and the honest wails of babies. They spoke of the wisdom of blood—veins, capillaries; of flesh and bone—brisket, tendons, ligaments, and skin. When some of the other boys in school started bullying me, I took to carrying one of the knives hidden in my dashiki. Pain was a sharp, ripping lesson those boys learned early on.

Still hanging in the imam's closet was a single Fulani robe. A shiny gray, it was symbolic of his office. Alone like that there was something about it that was both incongruous and melancholy. I felt the tears coming as I pressed my face into it and pretended I could still smell my father on it, even though my uncle must have worn it last. I pulled it over my head and it fell to the ground like a ballroom gown. I hitched it in my belt to keep from tripping, but still it swept the floor. I slipped one knife into the pocket of the robe and wrapped the others carefully and put them under the robe, tucked into the belt of my pants. With one last look at the empty house, I stepped out.

Barely a mile away, a man grabbed me. I didn't know what he wanted and I writhed like mad, trying to get away. I attempted to bite his hand but he delivered a stunning blow to my head. As I tried to grab my robe away from the man's clutches, my hand slipped on something hard and cold: the knife. I felt its sharp cut on my thumb goading me to action. I retrieved the knife; its gentle sag in my palm the weight of my decision. I struck. The first cut sliced off the man's finger, splashing surprised jets of blood onto his robes. A terrifying rage came over me and I slashed wildly, ripping gashes deep in the man's arms and face. It all seemed to happen in slow motion. There was blood everywhere. I broke free as the man convulsed and died. His face and arms crisscrossed with cuts. With a cold detachment that surprised me, I stuffed the bloody knife into one of my pockets.

I headed rapidly for the train station. The city center was

alive with mobs. Fires burned everywhere, some from Igbo-owned businesses, others from cars or piles of goods seized from the markets. There were even some Igbos tied to flaming crosses, their screams pitiful. The night sky was a red glow. It must have been at least midnight and yet both the old and new towns were alive with people like red ants crawling over a lump of sugar.

The ancient city was split into two distinct parts. The old city held the old sultan's palace, the central mosque, and the Islamic university, and was home only to the Fulani. Only they were allowed to live or conduct business in the old city. In fact, an infidel who so much as walked through there was courting death. The new city was called Sabon Gari—infidel's quarter. It was here that all the non-Muslims lived, conducted business, and had their churches. It was the commercial hub of the city.

I had to cross five miles of Muslim-controlled territory before I got to the trains. Soon enough, I was stopped by a mob.

"Who are you?" one of them asked me in Hausa.

"Sheik Rimi's boy," I replied, also in fluent Hausa. The Fulani backed off. Sheik Rimi was important, not only because he had the sultan's ear, but also because he was the feared ideological leader of the suicidal jihadic Maitasine sect. I only knew his name because my father hated him with a passion. Passion that was expressed in his use of the Arabic word walahi, and the way he used it, it snaked into the air and snapped back like a whip.

"Walahi! Fundamentalists will be the end of us all," he said.

I figured it couldn't hurt to use the sheik's name in this situation, and it paid off. For a while anyway.

"It might be dangerous to mess with one of his boys," one of the mob said.

"But up close, this one definitely looked like an infidel," another said, advancing.

"Prove it," the Fulani challenged. "Prove you are one of us and that the blood on your clothes belongs to an infidel dog and not a believer."

"How?" I asked.

"Sing the call to prayer."

In my best voice I began the call to prayer. A hush descended on the crowd as my voice went from a childish soprano to a cracked and smoky alto and then back again. The cracks teased some with memories of loves lost and dreams turned rancid. To others it was a caress that burned. Finally, unable to stand it any longer, a man screamed: "Stop! Somebody tell him to stop!"

The Fulani youth who stopped me initially pushed me roughly on my way. The rest of the trip to the train station proved uneventful. No one else stopped me. There was a train idling at the station and it was easy to sneak past the officials who were busy watching the mobs, onto the train, which was made up mostly of cargo coaches. Whatever they were carrying was very carefully held down with tarp. Ignoring the cargo cars, I headed for the one passenger car. It was empty and I hid in the toilet.

The journey down south to the nearest Igbo city of any significant size took thirteen hours. It was the longest, most harrowing trip I had ever undertaken. I kept expecting the train to stop at one of the many stations it rolled past and for the police or soldiers or an angry mob to pull me off and shoot me or eviscerate me. But there were no stops. The train was cheered at every station, town, and settlement it passed through and I guessed it had passed into Igbo territory when the cheering ended. A few hours later the train finally stopped, hissing angrily. I peered out of the window of the toilet, relaxing when I saw the sign on the platform. I was home.

I waited a few minutes before getting out of the train to be greeted by wails and screams of sorrow. The tarp had been rolled back to expose the cargo: dead bodies, hundreds of Igbo corpses, the harvest of a few weeks of carnage. Some of the bodies had started to decompose, filling the air with their rankness. Many were mutilated—vaginas, penises, mouths, noses, ears, hands, and feet were cut off or out. Even pregnant mothers hadn't been spared; their fetuses cut out and draped sickly over them. I turned away, retching.

I saw a group of men surround the Fulani train driver. He stood in their midst trying not to look scared, but his eyes gave him away. The first blow, when it came, was sudden and caught him off guard. He sank to the ground with a sigh. The blows that followed were swift and the only sounds were the fading cries of the driver, the soft thump of fists on flesh, and the gentle grunts of the men. In a few minutes they had beaten him to death with their bare hands. But the bloodlust was keen now and they were not sated. Seeing me standing mouth open, robes spattered in blood, they advanced toward me. But the women in the crowd formed a circle around me, a wall between the men and me.

"Step aside," the men said.

"So we are down to killing children now?" the women asked, not moving.

"They have murdered our children, so we must murder theirs," the men countered.

Just then I found my voice and screamed repeatedly. "I am Igbo!"

I throw my cigarette into the street and walk to the door of the bar. I stand just inside, signaling a request for food. I am an officer too, I think. I have led a platoon of mine diffusers, I have earned this right in blood; but they ignore me. Finally, an older man, graying, stands up and approaches me. He hands me his chicken. I am so clumsy, I let it fall. As I stoop to pick it up, he asks me if I have come for him. I shake my head, not understanding what he means.

"You are not a demon?" he asks.

I shake my head thinking all the old soldiers in this town must be shellshocked. I hear the other soldiers laughing about how the older man always sees ghosts and demons coming for him. I wonder why he thinks I am a ghost. How do ghosts appear?

Just then he raises his revolver. "Go now!" he screams.

I am already disappearing into the night when he fires. The bullet tears past me harmlessly. I hide in a bombed-out house further down the street.

"Crazy fucks," I mutter.

I am still holding onto the chicken.

I take a bite.

It tastes good.

A Thumb in the Air,
Clicking an Imaginary Lighter

This is what we were told: in the army, one mile is one click. It means nothing to us beyond army speak, so this is how we sign it: a thumb clicking an imaginary lighter held between fingers palmed into a fist. The number of clicks equals the number of miles. Simple really. I don't know how many clicks I have traveled yet; must be a lot though. I stretch in the early sun. The chicken last night was good but I am hungry again—however, if this town is full of old shellshocked, trigger-happy farts, then I need to leave. Still, there is no harm in trying to find another meal in the meantime.

The sun is high in the sky and the roads are melting from the heat, the tar coming away in sticky licorice strings with every step. Apart from a few die-hard traders and a record shop playing high-life tunes at full blast, there are only a few scraggy dogs lounging around, tongues lolling insanely, and I wonder if they are rabid. I decide not to take any chances and avoid them. Though the town looks deserted, I know it isn't. Everyone is just hiding from the possibility of a sudden blitz. I make my way to a decrepit and abandoned restaurant. Since I won't have any luck begging, I decide to treat myself to whatever I can liberate. I walk behind the counter, open the fridge, and help myself to a cold bottle of Coca-Cola. There is no electricity so the fridge must be kerosene-powered. There is some dry, weevil-infested bread on the counter and I wash it down with the Coke. Weevils are protein, I figure. The food and the sugar from the Coke give me a burst of energy. I decide to leave town. I already have so much ground to cover if I intend to catch up with my platoon.

I walk through the untidy spread. It is as though someone has thrown the houses down in a huff. The town is built on a slight hill and the houses look like spangles marching up the side of a doughnut. Glancing around, I guess I have stumbled on the poorer part because the houses have closely pressing walls of corrugated iron and cardboard and open sewers running out front. Here, children, naked, many sporting sores attended by tomb flies, run through the narrow alleys screaming in play, unafraid of bombing raids. There are no adults in sight except for a pregnant woman who lounges in one of the open doorways, cooling herself down with a raffia fan. I assume that most of the adults are either hiding or at work scavenging old farms or battlefields, trying to eke out a living. Life has to go on, war regardless.

I emerge into a leafier more salubrious neighborhood. It has taken longer that it would normally because I keep getting lost. I didn't intend to explore the town; I am actually looking for a way out. Here the houses range from old colonial mansions with rusting iron roofs to more recent mansions built by the new rich. Bougainvillea hugs nearly every wall.

I stop outside a high-walled house on a tree-lined street. Ornate gates open up onto a graveled path that sweeps up to a wooden colonial house. I know who lives here: the rebel minister for propaganda. This is where John Wayne stole his Lexus from. This is the house where I shot my first and only pregnant woman, the minister's youngest wife. I wasn't aiming for her, but for her husband, on John Wayne's orders, when she threw herself in front of him. All of us were shocked. That kind of love we had only seen in the movies, never in real life and certainly not in this war. It was a very strange moment for us. We had seen fathers shoot their children on our orders, sons rape their mothers, children forced to hack their parents to death—the worst atrocities—all of which we witnessed impassively. But this was different. We all cried when that woman died, except John Wayne, who was well lost. It wasn't dramatic really, just silent tears and a shame that kept us from meeting each other's eyes.

I approach the house from the back. Huge French windows, sans glass, open up onto a patio made from baked terra-cotta tiles. Giant tubs fringe it. Each has a small palm tree. I can't bring myself to enter, so instead I peer through the bare door frames. There are figures in the room talking. I must be dreaming, I must be because one of them is John Wayne, and if he is alive then I must be dreaming. I shot him. I know I am definitely dreaming when I see Ijeoma standing off to the left. She smiles sadly and says: "You aren't dreaming, My Luck, my love. These are memories. Before we can move from here, we have to relive and release our darkness."

I have no idea what she means. Does she mean I am going to die? Or that I am dead? I am pretty sure I'm not dead though, because that would make me a ghost, and I am pretty sure I would know if I was. There are known methods for determining things like this, I think. When I pinch myself it hurts, so I know I am not a ghost.

I turn and run back to the road. I walk for hours until I find myself back where I started. I stop at the record store and ask for directions to the next rebel-controlled town. I am sure I will find my comrades there. As I walk off, I beat a rhythm on my gun's stock. Playfully.

Child's Play

This is how we sign this: forefinger pointing to the sky while the whole body gyrates. For Ijeoma and me, play is a veiled thing, our own private language within a private language, sweeter for being secret. Rock, paper, scissors: one tap on our gun's stock, two taps, three.

One tap. One.

One tap. Two. A loss.

Two taps. One. A win.

Two taps. Two. A draw.

Endlessly we play, never looking at each other but smiling into the distance, hearts racing with the anticipation.

Then a steady hand, palm flat.

Silence.

Still we smile as we scan for the danger, our hearts beating:

One. One. Two.

Two. Two. Two.

Three. Three. Three.

A Hand Held like a Pistol

About a click outside of town, to my right, a steep bank of hills rises in green drama. Stunted trees struggle to hold onto the sheer faces. Creatures, maybe mountain goats, romp fearlessly at near ninety-degree angles. To my left the earth disappears into a deep ravine. Looking over the edge, I can make out a body of water. There is a scent in the air, a mixture of coriander, jasmine, and nutmeg that I know well: the smell of the savanna. That means I am approaching the middle plains. Closer to my home.

Up ahead the road passes alongside a large field. Set back on the far side are bleachers. This must have been the town's stadium. Red circles track the field like the grooves in a tree trunk. I pause and recall happier days before the war when I played soccer with friends in a league we made up. The cup was something fashioned from old wood, tin cans, and foil. Sharp thorns in the grass walls around the fields made it difficult as the balls were always bursting. The imam however approved of football and so I had a virtually endless supply of them. Of course, I would interrupt the games and take my ball home if too many goals were scored against me.

As I get closer, I see the sun has burned the field to a brown crisp. Here and there, patches of red earth spill through like giant puddles of blood. It is as though the very earth is peppered with sores. Scattered as far as I can see are corpses. Like a field of cut corn, cropped and lying in untidy rows, drying slowly in the sun. Further back, behind the bullet-holed stands, the trees straggle in an untidy shade.

A dark shadow, a cloud, hangs over the whole field. I stop and squint. The cloud is local and too dark for the sun to steal through. It is alive; moving; seething; humming. With a gasp I realize that it is a cloud of flies. The cloud heads toward me, then rears up, taking on a form, a huge black-winged angel. I rub my eyes. We've all heard stories about angels appearing over killing fields, but none so dark, so empty. The form dissipates as the flies spread over the dead like a loose cotton shift.

As I watch, I see phantom soldiers walking with bent heads, rifles across their backs. One soldier, perhaps sixteen, is shot in the stomach, a deep gash that spills his guts like sausages strung up in a butcher's window. He falls and I run to him, but a hail of bullets pushes me back. As I turn away, I see the boy stagger up and collect his intestines in an untidy heap, cradled like a baby in his arms. He then takes off, running. Desperate zigzag steps that send him crashing into the ground repeatedly, but he gets up every time. The shooting stops and I realize that it is phantom fire, and it isn't aimed at me. The ghosts are firing at each other—the rebels on one side and the federal troops on the other. But then everybody stops shooting and watches the boy; even the enemy. Twenty feet on, he just stops and sags, hitting the ground in a gentle droop. The backs of his legs are stained by his fear, but he still cradles his guts in his arms. He dies, mouth open. There is nothing heroic about it. This confuses me; can a ghost die? My jaw drops as another soldier looks up at me, eyes misty, transparent, mouth open in a smoke trail of speech. I shut my eyes tightly and shake my head. When I open them, the phantom soldier has gone. I scan the horizon; nothing. Then like mist, he coalesces again.

Suddenly a sword of lightning slices through the plumpness of the hot sky. Rain. I stand for a while but the hot rain is like molten lead and I flee for the line of trees behind the stadium, taking cover under one. I shiver in the new cold, debating whether the apparitions I have seen are real. In this place everything is possible. Here we believe that when a person dies in a sudden and hard way, their spirit wanders confused looking for its body. Confused because they don't realize they are dead. I know this. Traditionally a shaman would ease such a spirit across to the other world. Now, well, the land is crowded with confused spirits and all the shamans are soldiers.

I try to imagine what the imam would have thought about all this if he had lived. I realize that nothing I know of the world came from my Catholic mother or my Muslim father. All I know comes from the stories Grandfather told me. I feel a sudden rush of rage for father. What was it about Islam and the prophet and that way of life that made him

give up so much for it? He moved north, into the heart of
the place that destroyed us. What became of all those days
and nights he spent in fasting and prayer, rocking back and
forth in the dark and silent mosque that no one in the Sabon
Gari stepped foot in? What became of all those lessons he
taught me about the Koran and Islam? The five tenents? *All
Muslims must embrace no God but Allah and no prophet above
Mohammed, blessings be upon his name; all Muslims must at
least once in their lives perform the pilgrimage, the Holy Hajj,
to Mecca; all Muslims must pray five times a day, facing Mecca;
all Muslims must give alms to the poor;* finally, *all Muslims
must observe the Holy Fast of Ramadan.* Why didn't it say, *All
Muslims must never take another life, particularly one of their
own, particularly an imam—just because his wife is a Catholic
and his son, undecided?* That's what the Igbo press said, that
was the word on the streets in the Sabon Gari: *Local imam
murdered by other Muslims because he married a Catholic.*
Opus Dei, thousands of members strong, took to the streets,
singing in Latin, the Gregorian chant rising and falling like
a raven with clipped wings, a wonder to behold but unable
to fly. But the provocation didn't work; the streets weren't
filled with rioting Maitasine fundamentalists. A few hours of
marching depressively in the sun, and Opus Dei disbanded.
Of course, when the real pogroms started they didn't regroup
to fight, they fled. These were the people who murdered my
father, people from Sabon Gari. People he'd probably lent
money to. People who hated him as much as I do because in
the end, I know now, we always hate the saintly, the kind.

Not because they are kind, no, God knows we need that, but because their kindness makes us recognize the shits that we are. I fumble to light a cigarette. Beyond the shelter of the tree, the sky is an endless ocean and I feel like I am going to drown.

The old man I see approaching is like a lifeboat, pulling me back from that endless despair of sky. In his late sixties, small and wizened with the smile of a cherub, he is wearing a strange necklace of small bones with intricate markings. As he walks toward me, I see he is holding a sheaf of smoldering green herbs. The smoke from the bundle, thick and choking, wraps itself around the phantom soldiers, and as the smoke clears, the ghosts begin to disappear. He stops in front of me, head inclined. He is careful to keep the smoke away from me. He looks me over and introduces himself as Peter, the catechist of the church in the next town.

"But you look like a native priest," I say, though I must have thought it because we have no signs for these words.

He smiles: "The conflict is never in the truth, only in how we receive it."

"You are helping these souls."

He nods. "These spirits here are lucky. At least they are close to their bodies. Sometimes an explosion blows the spirit miles away from its body. Imagine how confusing that is."

The rain has eased to a hazy drizzle that wraps everything in a misty stole. Peter is standing about six feet away. I step toward him, the cigarette I hold out in offering between us.

He steps back. His expression doesn't change but something about him tenses. I stop. Does he think I am a federal soldier? Don't I look Igbo?

"I am not the enemy, you know," I say, but my hands don't move. We do have a sign for this kind of communication, mind to mind—telepathy is no stranger to us. A hand held like a pistol, forefinger as barrel and thumb as hammer, barrel swinging away from the forehead and swinging back.

He nods and squats. "We'll see about that," he says, drawing a sign in the dirt. "If you are a ghost, if you are dead, you cannot step over this sign." It is an invitation, a command almost. I smile and think this is just mumbo jumbo, but as hard as I try, I can't move. I don't know what to make of it. Just the power of suggestion, I say to myself, that's what all faith is, right? I realize that in my head I am talking to the imam.

Peter steps back and draws another sign, erasing the first with his foot.

"If you are a demon or mean me harm, you cannot cross this one," he says.

I step across it easily. He smiles and takes the cigarette from me. He says come and I follow, and although I feel his warmth like arms around me, he doesn't touch me.

River Is a Flat Snake

I stumble noisily after Peter who is moving with the grace and agility of a man half his age. I see the river rip out in front of me like a sudden sigh. I stop short. Peter comes back and pulls me along to the bank.

"I cannot go any further, I just need to close my eyes for a minute," I say, collapsing on the grass. "I am trying to find my comrades, my platoon. I am not a deserter, not a coward."

"I know," he replies. "Your friends are not far."

"You saw them?"

"They passed before you came onto the battlefield," he says, but there is something in his tone that makes me suspicious.

"Why is this river called the Cross?" I ask, since I can't put my finger on what is bothering me.

"Because we all have to cross it someday," he replies.

I shake my head. Why can't old people ever answer a question without using a riddle? I lie back on the bank. It feels like I have just closed my eyes when he is talking to me again.

"Wake up, young one," he says. "You can't stay here."

"You're right," I say. "I need to find my platoon. I am their leader, you know."

He smiles. "You look like a young general."

"Major," I correct, rubbing my eyes and coming up on one elbow. It is dark and I stare up at the stars pearling across the sky. I have lost all sense of time and don't remember night coming upon us. It seems like just a moment ago I was standing in broad daylight in a field of dead men.

"Your journey is almost over," he says gently. "You will need a boat."

I sit up and watch him push a canoe into the river. Everything comes back to this river, I think. Maybe Grandfather was right, there is no escaping its flow. As I approach the water, my hair stands on end and I hesitate. I can't do it. I can't row through the dead again. Not in the dark.

"Come on," he says again. Then reading my mind again, he adds: "You have all the light you need inside you."

It sounds like something Grandfather would have said. I don't believe him, but having no other choice I get in gingerly and push off, scything the water with the oars. I travel silently, disturbed only by the swish of the paddle. After a while, I pull the oars in, wrap my arms around myself, and settle back down to sleep.

I am still drifting downriver when I wake up. It is daylight. Stiff and sore, I look around. The thick forest has given way to large plains bordering each side. I wish I had some coffee; strong, sweet, and black. I gather phlegm and spit into the water.

The plains are man-made. Stumps point rudely where trees have been cut back. In some places, whole ghost forests hug the banks, trees half cut, dry, silver, and twisted. It has a tortured beauty. Before the war, the government gave grants to farmers on the plains to encourage and develop sheep farming. The amount of the grant was determined by the number of sheep each farmer had. People began to inflate the numbers of their sheep. To justify it, they began to annex part of the forest, cutting the trees back to develop more grazing land. But then the government twigged something was wrong and began to conduct inspections. To beat the inspectors, the farmers borrowed each other's sheep and drove them from field to field, always one step ahead of the inspectors. Pretty ingenious, I think; if it weren't so tragic. Now that the few hundred sheep have been eaten, all that's left is this barren forest, and a few abandoned structures, built like American ranches. I spit again. This was never really about farming at all. It was about a lifestyle. If peace ever comes, I hope it makes us wiser.

The rest of the trip passes in mental silence. A few hours later, I bring the canoe to a halt with a bump. I am back at the edge of the forest. *This fucking river and this fucking forest, I think.* I need to get home.

Right there on the bank, on the edge of the river, is an old fishing village. The houses are empty, roofs fallen in from neglect or from bombs, I can't tell which, but it's all the same, everything here is caused by the war. I sigh and pull the boat ashore, and hide it under some raffia from a fallen roof. I wonder who used to live here. So far, most of my stops have coincided with something that happened before. But I don't remember this village, or why I have been brought here.

There is a small lime tree, no bigger than a bush, right by the river. It is part of a row of stunted lime trees no doubt planted by the fishermen, the fruit used to clean and cure all manner of seafood. Plucking some, I crouch and throw one at a pot I see sitting on a cold hearth outside a hut. The pot falls over with a startled lid clatter, spilling rice which marches in an uneven column like termites. This excites some chickens scratching close to the forest edge. They dash over and peck merrily at the rice. The explosion I am expecting doesn't come. Next I lob another green grenade at a spilt basket. There is the crunch of a melon exposing its red innards. No explosion, which means no booby-traps. I stand up and walk toward the village. I am not worried about mines. If there were any, the animals would have either all died or left the village.

Methodically I begin to ransack the huts, looking for anything of value. Somewhere along the way I lost the bag of food I took from the stash in the forest clearing. The odd thing is, I don't remember when or how, and it is curious that I haven't come across another stash, but even odder is that I don't seem to care. Even as I work, I am disturbed by this invasion of other people's lives. In the sand by my feet are some black-and-white photographs of a family. I bend and pick one up. The mother, stern and well made up, stares stonily at the camera. The father has a sheepish grin. There is a baby, mouth open in a happy gurgle. Embarrassed, I drop it.

I find some palm oil, matches, salt, and spices. I stuff them into a raffia bag and stand, the bag hanging from one shoulder, my gun slung across the other, the bayonet, disconnected, tied to my boot. I light a cigarette, for the first time noticing the spent shell casings littering the floor like peanut husks. I look around me. There is a hill rising above everything in the distance. Probably the last part of the range I left earlier. Something that has been niggling at the back of my mind for days suddenly becomes crystal—I haven't heard the background rumble of mortar and shell fire for a while. What does it mean? I stub out my cigarette and head off.

I hack a path through the bush with a stolen machete, walking for hours, stopping to rest only once, to harvest some yams from an abandoned farm. It is late afternoon before I come upon the base of the hill. I climb to its flat top which spreads out like a green tablecloth spotted with warm yellow daisies and the blood of poppies, collapsing in a tired heap with an exclamation of pent-up breath.

I lie heaving gently in the backwash of the setting sun, all mauve and pink pastels. A valley dances misty-eyed way below, hiding the village in a cleft in the earth, a fold, sprouting a thick tuft of greenery, humping ever slightly like a pudendum. I light another cigarette from my never-ending pack and inhale deeply, the harsh smell cracking the beauty which reminds me of my childhood; of the first gulp of air

after I surfaced from my first time underwater for a few minutes, beneath Grandfather's alert watch. I wanted to take it
all into me and hold it there, indefinitely, teeth sinking in
startled gasps into its fudge sweetness, and yet it burned with
a pain that brought tears to my eyes.

As night falls again, I jerk back from the fire in which I
am roasting yams, howling from my burns as I haul one out
from the hot coals and onto a big green leaf. I cut it into
pieces with my bayonet and the heat steams up from the
chunks, misting the dark in soft white clouds. I thaw some
palm oil by the fire and crush salty herbs into it. I eat well,
and later I drink the sweet palm wine that I liberated from a
tapper's gourd tied to a palm tree trunk when I was digging
for the yam. The vanilla-scented liquid trickles down and
relaxes aching muscles, soothing away aggression and the
metallic knotted tension of living on the edge of death.
Leaning back and lighting a cigarette, I think about the
ghost soldiers and Peter's magic. What does it all mean? I
know this though: Grandfather used to say that the closer we
are to death, the easier our facility for seeing ghosts becomes.

Shelter Is Hands Protecting the Head

The lost manual would call for shelter, so I hunt across the hilltop until I come to a rock formation. There is a gap in the side. This is not a cave, but the space underneath two rocks, like the air pocket from a careless fold, is big enough for me to shelter in. It is not the leader's bunker, but then what is?

The leader's bunker is mythical. It is a talisman at its most ethereal, a mobile Camelot at its most concrete. Camelot: one of those things we learned in school that is useless to us now. Like the American Information Films that looked like they had been shot a hundred years ago, which were shown to us in boot camp. The films offered us ways to protect ourselves in the event of different kinds of enemy attacks, from catapults throwing Greek fire to napalm. There was one about protection in the event of a nuclear attack. It was simple and straightforward—hide under a desk. Some of those bush fucks in camp were impressed. Me, I could see through the fatal flaws of the logic even then:

1. Where would we find desks in this war?
2. Would the army provide them and would we have to carry them around ourselves?
3. Why would anyone hide from a fireball under a wooden desk?

But the frenzy of war dulls the senses. With death as our only option, I guess it is easy to believe anything. Besides, if the American government was telling their children to hide under desks, it must be true. They wouldn't risk the lives of their own children, would they?

I wish I had found this cave earlier when I was making dinner. That way I could have made the fire here and I would still have it to keep warm. This high, the heat from the day is lost very quickly and the rock feels cold against my back. I can always get up and go collect kindling and wood and build another fire, but I am too comfortable and tired to move. The best I can do is smoke. I light a cigarette and blow smoke out of the cave mouth. Is this how our ancestors lived so long ago? Hunter-gatherers making do in shelters like this?

In the dim glow from the cigarette, I try to see if there are any markings on the rock walls. I can't find any. Maybe I should make some. It occurs to me that this cave could be the result of a recent explosion, the force causing the crack.

I cannot remember how many days have passed since that initial explosion that separated me from my men. I should have made that mnemonic device, I think, absently stroking the Braille cemetery on my forearm. Stubbing out the cigarette, I shut my eyes.

Sleep comes easier and easier.

Sometimes rest too.

Music Is Any Dance You Can Pull Off

I have not returned to the road, though I can see it winding around the hill. Instead, I decide to follow a bush path down into the opposite foothills, rapidly descending to a valley. From the path, I can see for miles as I head down, my view obstructed only by the frequent clumps of trees and bushes that mark springs. The dust that coats all the vegetation by the roadside in a crumbly red ochre like an old villa wall doesn't seem to get this far, and the leaves here have a varied and beautiful appearance ranging from deep emerald, through mottled pink, ginger, and yellow, to a deep brown. The grass here is not high, no more than a few inches in places. There are patches where the sun has burned it, giving it the appearance of a heather moor. In the distance, herds of cows attended by young men and white egrets graze. The egrets stalk beside the cows in solemn procession, occasionally jumping on the cattle to feed on the fleas that hug their hide, or to wheel and cry like gulls in a display of dazzling whiteness. I stop and watch them, a song from my childhood, the song Grandfather taught me, coming back.

The terrain levels off for a while and I pass through some

more abandoned villages. The huts here are round. This gives the terrain the look of having haystacks dotted all over it. I go down one last steep incline and then the valley spreads out before me like a sheet. To the left, less than half a mile away, I can make out the silver ribbon of the river. Right in front of me, no more than a few hundred yards, is a lone house bordering a small pond. From somewhere I hear a gramophone scratch into life. It plays the same record over and over very loudly. The recording is of a voice; a woman's. No other instrument. The woman sings a bit like Marlene Dietrich but also a bit like Eartha Kitt. I know these singers from the movies we saw in boot camp. I almost wish for boot camp; anywhere would be better than this. I don't know what language the woman is singing in, it could be German, but as I follow the sound, which leads to the small tin-roofed bungalow by the pond, I am crying. It is dark when I finally arrive.

Outside on the veranda, in the soft light of a storm lantern, sits the gramophone and a man who looks to be in his late seventies. He glances up and sees me standing there and motions for me to join him.

"It's beautiful," he says, mournfully. "I don't understand a word but it brings a tear to my eye every time I hear it."

I smile, uncomfortable at his tears.

"I brought it back with me from the great war," he continues. "The gramophone and a few records were given to me by my captain for my part in liberating France from the Nazis. Now they've got all these new hi-fi's, but nothing plays like the old stuff. I don't know what the words mean myself, but I was told that it is a long slow lament for the Aryan race. I play it because the tone of the song is extremely sad, reaching down inside you and yanking at the parts of you best forgotten. Beautiful," the man sobs.

I sob with him.

"Are you okay?" he asks, after a while.

I nod.

"You don't say much."

I begin to sign my explanation, but he waves it away.

"It's okay, I have been alone so long I can talk for us both."

I smile and mime my thirst. He nods, and getting up he fetches a machete lying on the floor beside him. I point my gun at him, but he just laughs and walks to the edge of the veranda. He descends painfully and shuffles over to some banana trees growing beside the house. From a fallen trunk in the shade he cuts some small squares. Bringing them back, he hands them over.

"Suck on these," he says. "They'll cure your thirst in a way water cannot."

I suck gratefully. They taste salty, but surprisingly I feel my thirst slaked by the fourth cube. He then passes me some ripe bananas. They are so soft and ripe and sweet.

"You know, in the old days, in villages, banana groves were used as rubbish tips. The compost helped the bananas grow and the trees released a chemical that degraded the rubbish quickly whilst neutralizing the odor," he says. "I have survived on those bananas for so long I can't remember what real food tastes like . . . I am too old to hunt, you see," he adds, eyeing my gun pointedly.

I get up and head off into the underbrush. Minutes later I come back with a small antelope, not much bigger than a dog. I cut some banana leaves and quickly skin and gut the animal. He watches with eyes wet from hunger. When I am done, he takes the meat from me and disappears into the house. I can hear him talking as he begins to cook. I feel good. At least he doesn't treat me like a ghost. I lie back on the veranda and fall asleep.

The old man shakes me awake gently and places a plate of antelope stew beside me. We eat in silence and I can't believe how good the food tastes. I want to thank him, but in the darkness I don't know if he can make out my signs, so I don't. When I am done, several helpings later, I light a cigarette and pass it to him. He takes it and thanks me. I light one for myself. He gets off the veranda and goes to the banana grove and begins digging in the dirt.

"I play an instrument, but I keep it buried because of the war. I would like to play for you, to thank you for the meal," he says, grunting as he digs. I want to help him but I feel like it is important for him to do this himself. I wonder why he would worry about losing an instrument and not his gramophone, which would be more valuable to any passing thief. Finally, with a sigh he pulls up a square wooden box. Flipping it open, he removes a beautiful musical instrument. I have never seen one like it. Fragile, its body is made of a thin hollowed-out calabash, which acts as a sounding board. It is carved with designs and stained a dark color. A long neck curves up in an arc of brown obeche. It has strings arranged like a harp. He sits down on the wooden box, balances the instrument on his crossed knee, and begins plucking it with a fishbone plectrum, right there in the darkness of the banana trees. The sound is ethereal; disturbing; and I almost expect spirits to appear at his feet, dancing. The song is unrecognizable. It escalates and then, just before the crescendo of the final movement, it falls back into a sigh. The sound is tight and seamless and the tune seems to have been written for it. His playing ends on a soft note, which vibrates in the air for a few seconds afterwards. He opens his eyes and turns to where I am crouching in the darkness.

The moon tracks us in silver paint.

Roll Call Is Fingers Counting off a Palm

Roll Call—another chapter from the lost manual of John Wayne.

In my platoon there are only twelve of us left so there is no real need for roll call, as one glance takes in the whole group, but I am doing this for me. It hasn't been that long since I was separated from them but already their faces are unclear. I trouble the cemetery on my arm. This is an exercise in survival. I close my eyes and begin the roll call in my head, one that will include the dead, my fingers counting off in the air.

Ijeoma. She was the most beautiful woman I have ever seen. Skin dark as time-worn wood and smooth to the touch. Eyes that never turned hard, no matter what they were beholding, as if she had an infinite capacity for forgiveness. Teeth that stayed white and fresh from the stick that she chewed on almost constantly. It hung from the corner of her mouth like a cheroot in the old black-and-white movies I saw as a child. I remember she tried to smoke a pipe for a while, in the manner of the older female soldiers, but she kept choking so she gave it up. She had a laugh on her that was infectious, like the sudden pealing of a bell, and she was smarter than all of us. She would draw a circle in the dirt with a stick, and picking a star from the sky, she would chart the direction to follow. Even in the middle of the day, she could tell from the shadows what time it was, and she was the only one of us who understood the arcane markings on maps. How concentric squiggles were hills and how high they were. I miss her.

There was Nebu—short, stocky, and angry. Nebu never enjoyed killing, but for him it was his duty so he carried it out methodically and effectively. In a way, this made him seem more ruthless than the rest of us. This kind of dispassion was frightening to us. But he was dependable. A good soldier, and I felt sorry about the mine that just killed him.

Hannibal has a giant personality. For someone no bigger than a *Star Wars* Ewok, his laugh reminds me of a gorilla. He is also the practical joker of the platoon. He would bury defused mines under us while we slept and let us wake up to the panic that we were resting in a minefield. He also tied an arm or leg behind him and pretended to have lost a limb. He got us every time.

Isaiah is our prophet. He always wears an expression somewhere between the beatific and the deeply frustrated. I can understand that. In camp, before he lost his voice, he would quote from the Book of Psalms, and only the Book of Psalms, but our sign language was too crude for phrases like: *I have longed for your salvation, O Lord* (Psalm 174); *Mercies come unto me, that I may live* (Psalm 119); *He will never for-*

sake his children (Psalm 174); *How long Lord, shall the wicked, how long shall the wicked glory?*

American Express, or Amex, is the kid who can find you anything, anytime, and anywhere. He isn't one of us in the sense that he wasn't with us in boot camp and he doesn't diffuse mines. He is just a kid who has been following us for months now. He is only seven or eight, and in his bedraggled clothes that are several sizes too big, he looks like a scruffy elf. The .45 automatic he lugs around would be funny if it wasn't real.

Vainly I try to recall the rest but cannot. This is terrible and I feel caught somewhere between helplessness and guilt, betrayal even. How can I not remember people I have fought and died with over the last three years? People I have played cards with, played at soccer, danced with, pillaged villages with? What kind of leader forgets his men? Maybe that is why I cannot catch up with them.

I watch shooting stars like flares filling the sky.

Fingers Pinching a Nose Is a Bad Smell

Even before I see the camp, the smell of rotting bodies reaches me. It is a choking stomach-wrenching stench. I gag and hold my hand across my nose. Walking to the roadside, I pluck some aromatic grass from the verge. Crushing it into a field dressing I wrap it around my mouth and nose. When I breathe, a lemon-rosemary tang takes the edge off the worst of the smell. But it is still pretty strong and getting stronger the closer I get to the source. Monkeys call to each other and I stop abruptly as a family of baboons runs across the road in front of me. When they disappear in the forest, I continue.

I see the spire of the church before I see the makeshift buildings. When I round a bend, I see a temporary camp sprawled out in front of me. The camp is in a disused church compound and the forest has been cut back for at least fifty yards and a wooden fence rings it. And just beyond the fence, the river winds around. Everything is still a sparkling white except for where blood has stained some places black.

The sight that greets me is something out of one of the grisly fairy tales I heard as a child. On one side is a big pit dug into the earth from which flames leap maybe ten feet high. It is not clear at first what they are burning because there is so much smoke. Enough to hang like a blanket over everything. Near the pit of fire is a pile of dead bodies. There are flies everywhere, huge blue bottles that hum and dive like enemy planes on a bombing mission. I have to keep swatting to keep them off me. All over the camp, old women have lit bunches of aromatic herbs to drive away the flies and the smell of death, but the belching smoke from the funereal pyres smothers them and they are as ineffectual as an umbrella in a hurricane.

I realize what is going on. Some men are fishing the dead out of the water, others are throwing them on the growing pile, and others are chopping them up and feeding the parts to the flames. I know it is meant well; both to help the souls of the dead and to stop infection and disease from afflicting the living, but it is gruesome and frightening nonetheless. In fact, given that I have seen ghosts recently, I wonder if this is not hell and the people I see, demons. But there is something fundamentally human about them: the looks on their faces or the tired sadness in their eyes, I am not sure which. Some of them stop and watch me as I walk past. A new look has come into their eyes—fear? I want to assure them that I am friendly. I wave at them and continue past them and the pyre, heading instead for an outcrop of stone projecting over the water. I sit there, light a cigarette, and drag the smoke down deeply. Before me is the water heavy with a sun high in the sky. I imagine that in the past children would have played here, diving off the rock into the river below. It amazes me how this very river has flowed through my life.

I can't stay here, not tonight. I want to double back to the old man's place, but I need to press ahead, find my comrades. I flick the burning cigarette into the water and turn back to the forest. Still the river flanks me.

Dirty Is a Scrunched-up Face
and a Palm Waving

This river winds through my journey like an irritant that will not go away, and yet the water will not wash me clean. Not in a symbolic sense, but clean from the dirt here that grits every pore until I sweat mud. Neither will blood, though there is plenty of that to bathe in. It's not the stench, which after a while becomes bearable. It is the dirt: black soot from everything burning, dust and the loam of the forest, unwashed sex, blood and cordite, smoke, plant and grass stains, and mud for sweat. It all congeals into a second skin that still itches with its newness, like Adam must have felt as God first clothed his naked soul. When my fingernails rake, they first pull away thick flakes of it, then with repetition and increased pressure, skin, then more blood.

I stop by the river and light a cigarette. As I look around, the spot seems familiar. It is made distinctive by the big tree with bright red flowers that we call *flame of the forest*. They seldom grow this close to a river, preferring to hide deeper in the forest where hunters and startled villagers come upon its flame and are awed by it. It must have been years since we stopped here. Back then the war was only months old and I was still twelve going on thirteen and excited that my pubic hair was beginning to grow out. That's how you knew you were a man—pubic hair, then armpit hair, then facial hair.

We had made a stop to rest, the whole troop, vultures and all; plus a long train of refugees who had attached themselves to us thinking we could keep them safe. I had no idea where we were, but I didn't care. It was all still new enough to be exciting. Even then, the dirt was irritating and the vultures in particular. That band of soldiers who had to count the dead were already in the river trying to wash. My platoon and I were lying in the shade of the flame of the forest, and from that shelter I looked around me. Accompanying the refugees were some nuns—probably Irish, it seemed like all the Catholics here were—and they all wore that tight-lipped look that years of enduring Catholicism bestows on the pious, except for one of them. She was wandering around with a curious smile on her face. She looked unhinged. We turned and peered at each other and then back at the nun. We guessed that for her the dirt was more bearable than the debris that had no doubt collected in her mind, befuddling her. It was early on in the war, when the horrors were still new enough to unhinge decent people.

We watched her wander over to an outcrop of rock overlooking the river. She stood there awhile, the entranced smile on her face, and then without warning she leapt off. From that height the fast-flowing water below would be solid enough to knock her out and drag her under, delivering her into the ocean. For a moment though, it seemed like she was suspended in midair like a big black crow, her habit flapping like angry wings, before she disappeared, leaving behind a piercing scream.

Ijeoma shook her head. She was the first to speak: telepathy this time.

"The bird who made the world was like that. A big black thing with a white beak, and it flew over the face of the dark waters; it's screeching the first sound in God's memory, waking creation. Just like that."

We lit cigarettes, the whole platoon in one synchronized but unrehearsed movement, twenty of us in those days, and we sighed in a collective out-breath of smoke before returning to scratching from the dirt.

This dirt will not wash off with water.

Not even in a river.

What kind of God makes a world like this?

"Not God," Isaiah, our prophet, signed. "Man."

Ijeoma smiled.

"You know people," she said. Then she raised her forefinger to God and wiggled her body before bending down to pick up a pebble. Taking careful aim, she threw it at Nebu. We broke into play, throwing tiny pebbles at each other until we were a mass of small stings and lumpy bumps. We were flushed and breathing hard when we stopped, and grateful—for the pain that penetrated that skin of dirt.

On the outcrop of rock over the river, another nun prayed

for the suicide. In the distance, John Wayne was expounding on his manual loudly to a group of bored officers.

I return.

Now, sitting here, I realize that was important because it reminds me that even if water won't wash me clean, hope might.

A mosquito bites me. It is getting dark.

Cowardice Is Spitting Once

A wind sets to howling in the flame tree and I shiver in fear. I know it is the wind but it might also be disembodied spirits, or ghosts, or demons. The amount of blood on my hands doesn't grant me the luxury of complacence, and no amount of horror seems to have inured me to my own pain, or fear, or hunger, or desire. Only to that of others: war and its attendant deviance hasn't made me braver, only more callous. If any of my men could see me now, they would spit at my feet. The sign for cowardice.

The wind is calling in a voice I remember. A man John Wayne chased down into a woman's kitchen, a man unarmed and afraid, and John pulled him out and made him butcher his children in front of us. In that kitchen as though he would make a gory feast of them, as though he was a host and we his invited guests. And as that man chopped with the machete, blood spattering his face, I flinched from the greed in his eyes. The greed for living that made him do that, and then when he was done and panting from the effort, John Wayne put his revolver point blank to the man's head and blew his brains across the kitchen wall.

Tonight he is howling in the wind.

But I can't tell if it is anger, shame, or remorse.

Shit, I need to find my platoon. I cannot go on like this.

A Question Is a Palm Turning
Out from an Ear

If we are the great innocents in this war, then where did we learn all the evil we practice? I have seen rebel scouts cut off their enemies' ears or fingers or toes and keep them in tin cans as souvenirs. Some collect teeth, which they thread painstakingly into necklaces. Who taught us this?

Who taught me to enjoy killing, a singular joy that is perhaps rivaled only by an orgasm? It doesn't matter how the death is dealt—a bullet tearing through a body, the juicy suck of flesh around a bayonet, the grainy globular disintegration brought on by clubs—the joy is the same and requires only the complete focus on the moment, on the act.

Before the hate, before the war, I was in love with a little girl on my street, Aminatu, who gave me toffees from the jar on the counter in her mother's shop. I loved those toffees, always half-melted from the heat of her clenched palm and smelling faintly of her sweat.

I have never been a boy. That was stolen from me and I will never be a man—not this way. I am some kind of chimera who knows only the dreadful intimacy of killing. If it would help, I would cry, but tears are useless here. Anyway, I can't afford to lose any more fluids until I find clean drinking water. God, all this time and no water.

There are many ways to die in a war. Dehydration is one. For the want of water.

Vision Is the Same As Dreaming

I am in the middle of a battlefield.

The Angelus rings and I stop and lower my head. Before me, Ijeoma does the same. Behind us and all around but invisible in the shadows are the sounds of wings, a host of unseen. Ijeoma and I mouth the prayer together, lips folding greedily around words we can never utter: *The angel of the Lord appeared unto Mary . . . Hail Mary . . .* the words burn in us, like the love we still share. I finish and look up smiling.

Ijeoma is not smiling. Instead, she aims her rifle straight at my chest. I flinch at the report; flinch as the bullet tears through me. I feel my chest. No blood, no wound, nothing. Maybe it's a ghost bullet.

I look over at Ijeoma and now she is laughing. Silently, of course, but no less abandoned. I am in shock for a moment, then I drop my head back and howl at the moon. The hard convulsions of my throat, not the sound, wakes me.

I shiver in the dark. Something disturbs the fruit bats, maybe a python, and they scatter from their perches in the trees into the night, their wings like the sound of a hundred ghosts and their high-pitched squeals unbearable. It drives me to a deeper hysteria and I fire blind into the sound. Tonight the world is full of fallen angels.

A Train Is Forearms Back
and Forth Like Pistons

This village, nothing more than an old water stop for the train, is no more. All that I see is the rubble of some huts. There is only one standing—roofless, but humped there in the night, its protruding sticks and poles and crumbling earthen body give it the look of an elephant's skeleton. I pause by it, leaning against a pole. This trek of mine is getting more and more ridiculous, I think. I am mostly moving from one scene of past trauma to another, the distances between them, though vast, have collapsed to the span of a thought, and my platoon is ever elusive. I am thoroughly confused, but my desire—which is larger than my need to find my platoon, yet wrapped into it—is relentless in propelling me forward. I look at my watch. Ten minutes, it says. Ten minutes to or after, I cannot tell. Nor the hour; still, there is reassurance in looking at it.

I came here from the river, from that gruesome scene of brimstone, because while making my way through the forest, I heard the whistle of a train. If I can hitch a ride it should make my progress faster. But now that I am here I wonder if it is the right decision. Around me, darkness covers every-thing in a thick blanket of peppercorns. Occasionally the wind moves a cloud and the moon spills silver over the black. That's how I see the slow snake of the train approaching. By the time it reaches me, I am crouched by the track. The train moves slowly and it is easy to get a foothold and pull myself up. The cargo car I am now hunched in is empty, but I can smell straw and animals. Through the open door I can see more villages as we pass: huts crouching into the ground; orchards flowering in sweet scents; ponds; the river again; forests; more huts; a town with electricity, the neon some-how vulgar in light of the war, the music blaring in apolo-getic spurts; a straggly line of refugees walking, hugging the tree line, heading for some still distant hope.

The train begins to slow and pulls to a stop in a deserted station. Dawn is just ripping night's fabric, stars dropping as dew. A flickering storm lantern sways gently from the station-master's quarters, its light already diffused by the birthing sun. I know I have to get off here.

In the fragile sunlight, a woman is standing on the plat-form, scrutinizing the train. Her head jerks every time a door opens, but she turns away when she sees me and makes the sign of the cross. I cannot speak, and with her back turned she cannot see me sign, so I have no way of reassuring her. Something in the way she stands reminds me of myself, always searching for something.

I step from the platform onto the dusty road littered with tank carcasses like an elephant graveyard. When I turn back to look at the station, by some trick of the light the train has rusted over, the station fallen into ruin, and the bombed-out track coiled in on itself like spaghetti and covered in vegetation that crawls everywhere in a rush of green. I know it can't be true though, I just came from there.

Mirages are common here, I think, shaking it off.

Light Is Jazz Hands and a Smile

Out of a nightmare sometimes a good dream is born. Twice since she died I have met Ijeoma in dreams. Perhaps the third time will be in the afterlife. Walking in this silence, the solitude of early morning that in a different time, a better time, would be full of the ritual of coffee, a time when even songbirds are still, I feel alone in the world. Yet it is not a sadness I feel. This morning, unaccountably, I am filled with an almost unbearable lightness. This light comes not from a sudden wholeness on my part, but from the very wounds I carry on my body and in my soul. Each wound, in its particular way, giving off a particular and peculiar light.

I wipe my fingers across my eyes repeatedly, the equivalent of saying, *I don't believe it*, if I could talk. The road before me suddenly sheers away, ending abruptly in a cliff. I come to a halt on the edge and stare into an impenetrable darkness. There is something sinister about this particular darkness, as though every childhood fear I have is woven into its very fiber. I sit on a log by the roadside. Behind me, in the distance, I can make out the disused station and the rusting vine-covered train. In front of me is the darkness. I do what

I always do in moments of doubt, I light a cigarette. As I inhale, I think what a funny thing this habit has become. It is one I cannot do without and yet three years ago I didn't smoke. My parents (even my hated stepfather) would have gone berserk if they knew I was smoking. I remember a song I heard in boot camp, *War! Huh! What is it good for* . . . but instead of saying, *Absolutely nothing,* we'd add a phrase we like. I sing in my head. *War! Huh! What is it good for? American cigarette companies!* But it doesn't distract me for long and my mind returns to the anomaly in front of me.

I don't remember there being a cliff here. Not that I am sure I remember where I am, even though the sign at the train station was the same one I saw when I rode the train of death down from the north. Anyway, why would anyone build a road that leads to a dead end at a cliff edge? Apart from the obvious danger, it just doesn't make sense. I know the road wasn't bombed out because the darkness is too wide for any bomb we currently have. Only a nuclear bomb could do this much damage and I doubt either side has one, and even if we did and it had been used, the mushroom cloud would have been visible for miles, a tumor against the sky.

No, I decide, I am hallucinating. I must be. I scratch the cemetery on my arm and tell myself that if I put one foot into the darkness, it would disappear. I tell myself that this is only the shape of my guilt: guilt for all the lives I've lost or taken, guilt for letting my platoon down, guilt for losing my mother, for leaving her to die for me while I hid in the ceiling like a little coward.

I try to summon all the light that filled me moments ago. Light I need to cross the darkness. Still afraid and with no more light, I step over the edge of the cliff. The darkness vanishes and I am back on the road.

Ahead of me, a woman walks, a coffin balanced precariously on her head, her hips swaying with the effort, and yet poised, graceful even.

Mother?

Mother Is Crossed Arms Rocking a Baby

In thirty years, my mother's dreams had never lied. Though I only knew her for twelve of those years, and though she probably didn't mean them to, all her prophesies came true.

I know exactly when I began to think of her only in general terms. It was the morning of the day the imam died. Arising with dawn's fragile mist, she walked into the living room, straight to the sideboard that held all our photographs, and draped the imam's photograph with a black ribbon of mourning. I suppose you can say that my mother was a witch and in an older time, a rope around the neck would have tested her innocence.

This new prophesy came in the middle of the imam's latest fast and he had been in the mosque for days. It was inconceivable to either of us to tell him, to disturb his communion with angels and jinn. That morning as she went about the making of breakfast, her tears fell freely, if silently, over-salting the eggs and making the milk turn rancid so that the eucalyptus tea became undrinkable. If we were back in the south, with Grandfather, mother might have been able to work some counterspell, but the imam's faith forbade anything not of the one God, be it Christian or Muslim. For him, there was little difference, believing that both religions were brothers of the one father; a pair from the triplets—Judaism, Christianity, and Islam—a weird kind of trinity. But here, mother was denied even the mercy of a dried chicken heart that when clutched in a cooling palm could be used to ward off demons, so she spent that day watching in silent terror their bald-headed approach. Now I wonder if she was crying also for the more distant future she saw coming. If I blamed her, *blame* her, I blame the imam equally for his own death. The seed of it was his greatest arrogance, the belief that he knew the will of the unknowable. Grandfather always said that believers are like unschooled children holding onto the essence of a truth merely because they have spoken it. But now that I have seen a soul all brittle and flaky like coughed-up biscuit crumbs leave a man, blame is not so easy to lay on another.

All that day and into the night, my mother knelt before her altar, before the icon of the Virgin, before the candles burning, and rolled her rosary between her hands, beating her chest and calling for mercy, for some intercession. As I watched her, I realized that she could see death, and I too, and it wasn't some ugly skeleton with a scythe—death is a beautiful woman, eyes soft from morning dew, lips pulled back in the saddest smile, praying at an altar for her husband's life.

When it grew dark and mother didn't move from her vigil, I finally decided to do something, and headed to the mosque. Whatever the consequence of waking him, death must be more extreme, so I lit a candle and stepped out of the house. In the alley between the mosque and our house, my fear smothered the candle flame and the darkness crackled in the heat. It was early but the streets were deserted. I entered the mosque from the side door, walking quickly through the courtyard that housed the ablution fonts, the sand crunching under my shoes. Not bothering to take off my shoes, I ran across the mats to where the imam lay face-up in a trance. I shook him and shook him, but I couldn't wake him. Then there were two shapes beside me, each holding a sword. As they raised them to strike, I ran, like a coward, I ran and hid in the courtyard, behind the farthest font. I heard the imam cry out, and then stumble out into the courtyard, chased by his assailants, who cut him repeatedly. When they fled, I came out to him. He smiled at me and touched my face, smearing his blood on my cheek. He tried to speak, but only blood came. I pushed back from him and he died in the sand like a dog.

Oh, how can my sin be so luminous!

I ran back to Mother. She was waiting with a bowl of water and a rag and she washed my face and said nothing. Instead, she just held me and rocked back and forth singing softly: "You Are My Luck."

I scream, or try to, but the sound that comes from me is no more than a harsh gurgling like a wild animal dying. I fall to the ground. The woman ahead of me pauses, turns, and sees me. It is not my mother. She puts her coffin down and walks back. She squats beside me, and holding my head up she pours water from a canteen into my mouth.

As I struggle to drink through my choking, she strokes my forehead and whispers: "Son."

Rest Is a Chin Held in a Palm

"Death is our burden to carry," the woman says, when I point to the coffin and raise my eyebrows. The water she gave me has revived me and I am sitting up, propped against the coffin, smoking another cigarette. I offer her one, but she shakes her head, reaching into her bra and pulling out a small round silver box with a mirror on its lid. She taps it a few times, twists the cap off, and dips a moistened forefinger into it. It comes out packed with snuff, which she rubs against her gums. She makes a satisfied sound, tears running from the harsh hit. She turns and gives me a watery smile. I look away. I have a persistent hunger, an appetite for something I can't define. Above, the sky is becoming overcast.

"We should find shelter before it begins to rain," she says.

I nod and get up. I look down the road. There is a bamboo grove not far. I guess the river winds back at that point. Bamboo clumps grow on the banks and droop like willows, rippling fingers through the dirty water. Grandfather said they were mermaids who while washing their hair didn't notice the gaze of humans until too late. They became

frozen, the bamboo all that was left of them, still vainly trying to wash their hair in the river. It should be easy to build
a shelter there. I turn to the woman.

"What is your name, Mother?" I sign, using the respect-
ful term for a woman old enough to be my mother. It is the
way here. She likes it, she smiles.

"My name is Grace," she says.

"Come, Mother," I sign. "We can find shelter ahead."

She helps me hoist the coffin onto my head and we move
along. It is natural and fitting that I should take the coffin
from the old woman. I am stronger and younger, yet I feel
even closer to death with the infernal box on my head. Grace
says nothing, just follows. When we get to the grove, I clear
the ground shrub just away from the road, the blade of the
machete fast against the hollow bamboo, sounding a song of
steel and wood. In no time I have built a lean-to and roofed
it with bamboo leaves woven into small squares; and just in
time because I have barely hauled the coffin into the shelter
when the sky opens up in a storm.

"Can you build a fire?" Grace asks.

If she thinks it is strange that I don't speak, she has said
nothing. I nod and gather kindling. It is easy—I just reach
back into the grove. Soon there is a small but cheerful blaze
going. Grace opens the coffin and pulls out a pot and some
cooking ingredients. As she stands the pot in the rain to collect water, she asks: "Is that yam I see in your bag?"

I nod and offer it to her. She peels it quickly with my
bayonet, her grip experienced, and then she holds it out in

the rain to wash it clean. She chops it and puts it in the pot of water, adds the last of the oil from my bag, some herbs she has, and a piece of dry fish she has been clearly hoarding for some time. While we wait for the rain to abate and the yam pottage to cook, I smoke and she rubs snuff on her gums. She begins to talk.

"I've carried this coffin for so long, for such a long time. You see, we are nothing if we don't know how to die right. That sums us up as a people. Not the manner we come into the world, but the manner in which we leave."

After all that I have seen, it sounds a little self-indulgent, but it's not like I can interrupt her, so I let her go on. It seems important to her to tell me this stuff, although I don't know why. Why, even in moments like this, do people feel they have to explain their oddness? If no one felt that kind of shame, that kind of embarrassment, would there be no more war? It sounds silly. I guess this is what Grandfather meant when he would say I was acting my age.

"One day I will die and then my killers will be able to bury me easily."

I want to laugh but it would be unkind.

"I even have a headstone in here," Grace continues, pointing to the coffin. No wonder it is so bloody heavy, I think. But she isn't too irritating and I am grateful for the company. Besides, the food smells great. She busies herself dishing it into earthenware bowls she digs out of the coffin. A right Pandora's Box, I think. We eat in silence. I remember her taking the bowl from me, but nothing else.

When I wake, she is gone. Like the rain and the bamboo grove. In fact, I wake up in the coffin beside the river, quite a distance from the grove. I leap out. She must have moved me, but how, and why? What kind of sorcery is this?

Just then, across the river, I catch sight of Nebu and the rest of my platoon. They are resting on the opposite bank. I scream and wave but I think I am too far away because they don't act like they've seen me. There is nothing else to do but cross the river. I have no boat, so I push the coffin into the water. Shuddering, I get in and begin paddling with my arms.

Fear Is an Open Hand
Beating over the Heart

There are many things about John Wayne that I despised, but this I admired: the man had no fear. It was almost as though the word, or the concept, was foreign to him. He was obviously too old and big to be a mine diffuser, but he was always up there at the front with us, risking his life, spraying the enemy with his weapon of choice, the squat ugly Israeli Uzi.

"The perfect weapon," he would say. "Not much to look at, easy to handle, and deadlier than anything else out there. Like me." This was followed with a big laugh, the kind of head-thrown-back, I-am-full-of-life laugh. Sometimes he would have a bottle of beer balanced precariously on his head and he would forget and throw his head back, sending the bottle crashing. These are the sounds that remind me of him: the high-pitched metallic spitting of his Uzi, the deep laugh, and the sound of breaking glass.

I remember one time a few weeks after we had just left camp; we were pinned down by heavy enemy fire from a gun we would later know as the M60. While all the other platoon leaders were hiding or taking cover, John Wayne spotted the gun encampment and, standing up, he ran straight for it, stopping less than ten yards from it to throw three grenades. As he hit the deck, the explosion sent bits of gun and men flying over him.

"There are only two things a man should fear," he told me once. "God and women. That's all." Then he laughed; John Wayne a.k.a., Major Essien. Now I know he couldn't have been a real major. Majors don't lead platoons, lieutenants do. I wonder why I kept him out of my mental roll call that night.

The only other person who seemed immune to fear was Ijeoma. Maybe it is no coincidence they are both dead. Now though, as I embark across the river of the dead in a coffin, I wish for some of their fearlessness.

It is useless; I am shivering like a wet cat.

Will Is an Emphatic Finger Pointing

The coffin spins around like a leaf turning in an eddy. No matter how hard I try to paddle, it keeps spinning in the same place, midway across the river.

Frustrated, I shoot my gun into the air until I run out of ammo and the trigger just clicks, the hammer echoing metallically. Sobbing, I watch as my platoon gets up and heads off, into the forest. They don't see or hear me. How is that possible? I'm not that far away. *Fuck this war*, I think. *Fuck it all.*

Tired; I am so tired. I give in and lie back in the coffin. So tired; too tired.

As I drift off to sleep, I feel the coffin drifting toward shore.

I don't care anymore.

Home Is a Palm Fisted to the Heart

It is late evening when the coffin finally bumps up against the opposite shore. Wearily, I climb out. There is a house on the bank and all the lights are burning. I drop my gun and my bayonet and my machete. I am too tired, I can't do this anymore. If death is what awaits me, I want to face it without fear. I've had enough of that.

There is a woman sitting on the veranda on a porch swing. She is young and smiling and happy. As I approach, I realize who she is. It can't be, but it is.

My mother looks toward me and holds out her arms. I stumble into them and she pats me on the back.

"My Luck, My Luck," she says. "You are home."

I pull back and look at her. I am trying to make sense of it, to think, but I can't focus.

"Mother," I say, and my voice has returned.

Acknowledgments

My thanks to: Percival Everett, Cristina Garcia, Sarah Valentine, Steve Isoardi, Jeannette Lindsay, Peter Orner, Brad Kessler, Dave Eggers, Johnny Temple, Johanna Ingalls, Ellen Levine, Beth Shube, Ron Gottesman, Kachi Akoma, Rebecca Brown, Titi Osu, Matthew Shenoda, Anna Silver, Elaine Attias, Nick Rosen, Miguel Atwood-Ferguson, Joey Dosik, and Elias Wondimu.

My family.

All my friends.

Also from AKASHIC BOOKS

BECOMING ABIGAIL by Chris Abani
A selection of the *Essence Magazine* Book Club
and Black Expressions Book Club
128 pages, trade paperback original, $11.95

"Compelling and gorgeously written, this is a coming-of-age novella like no other. Chris Abani explores the depths of loss and exploitation with what can only be described as a knowing tenderness. An extraordinary, necessary book."
—Cristina Garcia, author of *Dreaming in Cuban*

SHE'S GONE by Kwame Dawes
340 pages, trade paperback original, $15.95

"Dawes offers vibrant characters and locales, from Jamaica to the American South to the Urban North, in this diaspora of black culture and strong emotions, bordering the fine line between love and madness between two troubled people."
—*Booklist*

THE GIRL WITH THE GOLDEN SHOES
by Colin Channer w/an afterword by Russell Banks
172 pages, trade paperback, $12.95

"A jewel of a book . . . Channer's language is juicy, his humor incisive, his vision penetrating, and his hero, nicknamed Pepper for her stinging retorts, is magnificent."
—*Booklist* (starred review)

Selections from Chris Abani's poetry imprint
BLACK GOAT

 **GOMER'S SONG poems by Kwame Dawes**
72 pages, trade paperback original, $14.95

In *Gomer's Song*—a re-rendering of a Bible story—
Dawes examines the insidious nature of power, the
expectations of gender roles, and the limits of protest
This is a tender book with profound lyrical insight.

 **AUTO MECHANIC'S DAUGHTER**
poems by Karen Harryman
84 pages, trade paperback original, $14.95

"Charting the vicissitudes of her own life, and the
travails and triumphs of those whom she knows
and loves, Harryman travels great distances in her
poems."
—Maurya Simon, from the introduction

 **EEL ON REEF poems by Uche Nduka**
152 pages, trade paperback original, $15.95

Award-winning Uche Nduka challenges every
expectation of an African poet. His unique voice is
a heady amalgam of Christopher Okibo, A.R.
Ammons, John Ashbery, Kamau Brathwaite, and
something only Uche can bring.